Paul Breen

Hugh O'Nell's war with Queen Elizabeth, Irish national effusions and

miscellaneous poems

Paul Breen

Hugh O'Nell's war with Queen Elizabeth, Irish national effusions and miscellaneous poems

ISBN/EAN: 9783337118389

Printed in Europe, USA, Canada, Australia, Japan

Cover: Foto ©Andreas Hilbeck / pixelio.de

More available books at **www.hansebooks.com**

Very Respectf.

C. J. Bre...

HUGH O'NELL'S WAR

WITH

Queen Elizabeth,

IRISH

NATIONAL EFFUSIONS

AND

Miscellaneous Poems.

BY

P. C. T. BREEN.

CHICAGO:
CLARK & EDWARDS, PUBLISHERS,
1882.

INTRODUCTION.

In stepping forth from the calm surroundings of modest retirement, into the expansive dominion of literature, I find myself accompanied with the peaceful reflections of an unassuming mind, thirsting not for the honor and glory of fame, but with an undying love of nationality; that the fire of my humble genius may add to the brilliancy of the unextinguished lamp of patriotism, which ever burns within the sublimity of holy aspirations of freedom—as immortal beacon lights of victory, leading to glory the undaunted sons of heroic sires who were never destined to fill a bondsman's grave.

In bringing before my readers the illustrious chieftain of the house of the Hi Nials—the valiant Hugh O'Neill, I have attempted, though feebly, to portray the master genius of that military hero, as he stood in proud defiance on the lofty pinnacle of fame, sweeping into oblivion, the tried, trained generals, of the British army with the invincible prowess of his herculean arm, as he stood forth in the arena of conflict, inspiring his soldiers with heroic deeds of action, that his own beloved Erin might be disenthralled from the polluted influences of a tyrannical government, which has always tried to crush beneath the force of its steeled barbarity, a race, too proud, too honorable, too brave to be contemned. The glory of his invincibility shall live forever in the monumental recollections of his fame, and inspire the minds of all untainted with the pusillanimity of slave-born proclivities, to die in the struggle of freedom's holy cause, before the shackles of serfdom should plow deep into the limbs of a brave and glorious people.

The spirit of modest song, which breathes through the Irish National Effusions, however humble, instills a love nationalistic suavity within the soul which throbs with the pulse of freedom. When the recollections of homes sweet early scenes spread themselves before the minds eye, with all those endearing charms which

INTRODUCTION.

nature, with unstinted lavishness bestows upon them, is
it a matter of surprise, that a heart estranged from those
associations should awaken from the solitude of its neglected love, when touched by the fire, not perhaps, so
much of poetic genius, as the subject matter itself, bringing its realized sublimity of sweetness into the very soul
from which it was so long estranged. If this should be
the case, and I could feel that my humble writings were
productive of national aspirations of freedom, then the
hours of sweet communion with the muse, which filled
my soul with song, should ever cast their pleasing recollections around me, with a peaceful assurance of delight, as the ,wintry blasts of life chill my brow with
decaying old age; for

> Next to God's glory alone,
> Our country should always be given
> The dearest affections we own.

The Miscellaneous Poetry, which is largely made up
of incidents of local surroundings, which more or less
attracted my attention, has a peculiar interest for myself, through the association of friendly relationship
which gave them birth in my humble stanzas. The
mind of the poet, though holding secret converse with
the muse, and wrapt up in the sweetness of her inspiration
still finds itself courted by those passing events, which,
in social intercourse, flow down the tide of life together
into the unfathomed gulf of eternity; and though the
subjects may be uninteresting to some, yet those ties of
friendship, which knit together the peaceful remem-
brance of other days in the poet's mind, will, I hope,
awaken the heart of the gentle reader to a thoughtful
reflection of forgiveness, and ascribe the fault, if such it
be, to the affections, which social companionship nursed
in the soul of

P. C T. Breen.

DULCE ET DECORUM EST

PRO PATRIA MORI.

TO THE
HONORABLE
CHARLES STEWART PARNELL,
The illustrious Irish Nationalist,
The eminent statesman,
Whose name and fame
Shall ever claim
Immortal honor and renown
Far brighter gems than ever yet
Bedecked a monarch's crown
This little book as an
Echo of Ireland's
National l o v e
for thee
Is respect-
fully
Dedicated.

INDEX.

―――o―――

HUGH O'NEILL'S WAR

WITH

ELIZABETH.

HUGH O'NEILL.

———

Hugh O'Neill, the illustrious chieftain of the House of the Hy Nialls, who governed over Ireland as Monarchs for a period of about seven hundred years, accepted from Elizabeth the title of the Earl of Tyrone in order to avoid the suspicion of the English during his occasional visits to England. Though always appearing to act in the interests of the Queen, he studied every advantage which afforded him an opportunity of increasing his own knowledge, until he had thoroughly acquainted himself with their tactics. By this means he became an accomplished tactician.

He organized an army of six thousand men in his own province and secretly instructed them in the use of arms, uniting at the same time the discipline of both countries in the course of their experience. The Irish were complaining of his inactivity in consequence of his not joining immediately the standard of revolt raised by O'Donnell, who had made his escape from imprisonment in Dublin Castle with two other northern princes. But as soon as an opportunity favored his designs, he renounced the title of Tyrone (A. D. 1595), and declared war against the Queen, in conjunction with the Maguires, McMahons, Maginissis, McDonnels, and other illustrious chieftains who espoused the cause of poor bleeding Ireland.

Hugh O'Neill became their Commander-in-Chief and honored the cause with immortal renown.

HUGH O'NEILL'S WAR
WITH
ELIZABETH.

No more shall the title of Earl disgrace
The ancient renown of O'Neill's gallant race,
The mighty Tyrone has assumed his own name,
No false colors shadow the light of his fame;
In his own native land, like Hector of yore,
The foeman's proud standard of battle he bore;
The might of his valor triumphantly rose
And chilled in his presence the hearts of his foes.
The chieftains of Erin beheld with delight
The great Hugh preparing his men for the fight.
The free loving Bess, like her amorous sire,
Had kindled the war flame with wanton desire;
Since the sad invasion of England began
No greater resistance was made to a man.
The Irish, like crested Acheans, were seen
Brave, calm and determined, all glit'ring with
    sheen.

The tyrantess vow'd from her bloody stained
    throne
She'd humble the pride of the mighty Tyrone,
And leave not one spark of the old faith to burn—
The ashes of papists she'd place in one urn.
With fierceness of action she issued commands
Recalling her old troops from the Netherlands,
To Norris* the command of th' armies she gave
To render old Erin a vast purple grave.
With ten thousand men in the land of the Geal
He swore he would capture the rebel O'Neill;
Yet, soon as he landed he lost the intent,
A white flag with tidings to the chief he sent,
Requesting a truce from the brave gallant Hugh
To try what a peaceful commission could do:
The truce was agreed on, yet peace stood afar,
The wild echoes answered the trumpets of war.
The armies on both sides nursed silence as dread
As the solemnness keeping the shades o' the dead.
The deputy, Russel, with his army corps
When marching for Armagh unceasingly swore,
The clans of the Irish he'd sweep like a blast

* Sir John Norris, former Gov
Commander of the English Army in the low countries, against the
King of Spain, was considered one of the best commanders in Her
Majesty's service.

As Boreas splinters the lofty main mast.
The voice of bravado had scarce died away
When the hosts of Erin in martial array
Were seen in the distance, with banners of
    green,
Ignoring the power of the 'Sassanaugh Queen.'
On the plains of Kilona the battle began—
Jove-like, majestic, the O'Neill leads the van;
His voice like a trumpet was heard o'er the
    plain—
Charge! Charge on the Saxons; your glories
    maintain.
As a fierce mountain flood o'ercharging its
    banks
The Irish rush down on their enemy's ranks—
The invading forces, with tempest-like rage,
Imbued with destruction, as fiercely engage.
The dark, frowning war-clouds of terror are
    there,
Like storms, growing fiercer in the midnight
    air,
Contending with dark, rolling flames rushing
    high
From the lap of destruction, where crashing
    walls lie.

The contending armies thus fiercely contend,
The sabre and pike with their dread issues bend,
The Irish 'repressible appeared in war,
Whilst clanking of weapons resounded afar,
The dauntless O'Neill in the vanguard is seen,
With eyes flashing light like his broad sabre's
    sheen;
His brow looks as fierce as the great moun-
    tain god,*
Depicted as shaking the earth with his nod,
O'Cahon, O'Hanlon and fearless Maguire,
And other brave chieftains their soldiers inpsire
With terrific cheers for their loved native shore
Through the British ranks with dread ven-
    geance they tore.
The cohorts of the stranger, like broken reeds,
    yield,
O'erpowered by the Irish, they fly from the
    field.
Their dying and dead overshadow the plain,—
With terrors arising from so many slain,†
From Ulster, the deputy made his retreat,
Dejected with sorrow at such a defeat.

---

*Olympian Jove.

†The English were compelled to retreat to Newry, after leaving
six hundred men dead on the field. O'Neill lost about two hundred
men on that occasion.

He ‡ gave up his soldiers to Sir John's com-
mand,
Too fearful of meeting the chiefs of the land.
The banner of Ulster waved high 'bove the
trees,
Extending its soft silken folds to the breeze;
The brave sons of Erin had dared to unfold
That emblem of freedom and glory of old—
That freedom so holy, so precious, divine,
So long lost to Erin—yet, Erin 'twas thine.—
To restore their lost rights, and wipe out the
stain
Of England's pollution, the chiefs met again.
Lord Deputy Russel's defeat cheered them on.
With bright hopes, increasing the glories they
won.
They marched to Cluoin Tiburuid with speed
like the roe,
To slacken the pace of the retreating foe.
Where a small winding stream there indents
the plain
O'Neill raised his standard with proud lofty
mien;
Then, calling around him the chiefs of his race,
With joyful expressions of hope on his face,

‡A great deal of jealousy having existed between Sir John Norris and the Lord Deputy, about the command of the armies, a disunion existed between these gentlemen until the latters ill success in
his first encounter with O'Neill. when he gave up his command to
Norris. and returned to Dublin in disgust.

He pointed his sword where the proud Saxons
  stood

Then spoke he: "that stream shall run red
  with their blood;

Our Faith they have trampled, our virtue
  reviled,

The graves of our fathers' for years they've de-
  filed,

Our wives, mothers, sisters the old and the
  young

They've shot without mercy—they've shamefully hung.

Prepare then to meet them; deal death to the
  foe;

Make England's base hirelings remember the
  woe;

They've heap'd over Erin with wanton delight,

Engulfing her beauties in horrors' black night."

The dread echoes answered the shouts of his
  men

And bore them with terror through mountain
  and glen,

Like the pealing thunder's vibrations in air

When dark clouds are riven with tempests'
  despair,

And strong men like aspen leaves tremble and
  pale,

Thus England's hosts 'waited the Sons of the
    Geal.
General Norris o'ercharg'd with their spleen,
Rode frantic with fury exhorting his men
To strike down the papists with merciless hands,
And leave not one rebel to cumber the lands.
With fierceness, like tigers awaiting their prey,
They stand for a moment in martial array,
Impatient with vengeance growing dark on each
    face—
Then head long they rushed to wipe out the old
    race.
The soldiers of Erin with proud defiance,
Met their fierce shock with that calm self-re-
    liance,
Which breathed the spirit of God's strength
    alone,
With grand human efforts to die for their own.
The contest grew dreadful, the stream flow'd
    with blood,
And delug'd its banks with its impurpled flood;
The chieftains engaged in the battle with might,
Resolving to conquer or die in the fight.

A brave British officer* fought well that day,
Like Ajax. he felled all obstructing his way,
Until he encounter'd O'Neill in the van,
Inspiring with valorous deeds his brave clan,
A dark frown of vengeance, with spectre-like
      dread,
Overshadow'ng the graves of the mold'ring
      dead
Swept over the brow of the Britain so bold,
Who dared to encounter the Red Hand of old.
The god-like O'Neill with his ponderous lance
Poised high in the air toward his foe did ad-
      vance;
The ground seem to shake with the force they
      display'd,
When a contest of strength in the action was
      made.
The armies stood still as if death's shadow'ng
      spear,
Benumb'd the existence of each man with fear;
The sight of their Chieftains in combat en-
      gag'd,
Filled 'em with awe as if the gods battle wag'd.

_____
* Segrave, an officer in the army of Norris, fought his way to
where O'Neill was, and encountered that Chieftain in single combat.

Segrave with the strength of a tiger began
To hurdle his spears at the great Irishman,
Who warded them off as his own sped away,
Commission'd with might the bold soldier to
    slay.
Two lances were shattered by each chieftain
    brave,
But yet, no cessation would either dare crave—
Then clenching their broad swords with eyes
    flashing fire,
They renew'd the contest with dreadful desire.
O'Neill made a thrust at the breast of his foe,
But Segrave, as valiant, parried the blow,
Then sprang like a wild beast, with one fearful
    yell
To cut down the papist and send him to hell;
His sword in a moment descended through air,
With fury denoting the wrath of despair;
It rang on the steel of the chief of Tyrone,
With a harmless clang breathing vengeance
    alone.   •
The hero of Ulster with grave calmness said
Thy life-blood this day shall yet flow with the
    dead;

The dark, grim shades of Mors, thy manes shall
    hide,
My broad sword shall humble the freebooters'
    pride—
Like a tremendous oak, whose ponderous limbs
Betoken the strength of its earth clasping
    stems
Crush'd down by the shock of electric fire,
Thus Segrave fell clothed in bloody attire.
Loud shouts of triumph from O'Neill's gallant
    band,
Awakened the echoes of fame in the land;
The ranks of their foes grew disordered and
    fled,
Leaving behind them their dying and dead.*
Monaghan surrendered, on the following day
To the Clans of Ulster in martial array,
The force of their pow'r overshadow'd the
    throne,
Like the mystic writing Belshazzar had known.
Elizabeth, fearing O'Neill's sweeping pow'r,

---

* The English lost seven hundred men in that dreadful battle
field ; the Irish not one-third that number. On the following day,
the garrison at Monaghan surrendered to O'Neill ; he allowed them
to march out with the honors of war.

(Though wishing she had him enclosed in the
    tow'r),
Declared she would pardon him if he'd lay down
His claymore and stand in defence of her crown.
The brave gallant chief with a proud haughty
    smile,
Thus answered the foe of his dear native isle:
My sword in its scabbard shall never be seen,
'Till freedom is pledged to old Erin the Green.
The pow'r of " Queen Bess " I shall ever defy,
Go tell her, Sir Edward,* I fear not to die;
Her pardon I seek not, no favors I crave,
Instruct the usurper—O'Neill 's not a slave.
The bold fearless tone of the chieftain's demand,
Inspired the proud princes all over the land
To unsheath their swords, and to battle with
    pride
For freedom for Erin, with Hugh by their side.
The chieftains of Munster threw off their dis-
    guise,
The famed clans of Connaught extoled to the
    skies

---

* Sir Edward Moor was instructed to offer the Queen's pardon
to O'Neill in 1596, if he would lay down his arms, but that undaunted hero refused to accept her terms of peace, deeming her a
usurper of the rights of Ireland.

The heads of their Septs ever faithful and bold,
When called on, their own beloved flag to up-
    hold.
King Philip † had promis'd their cause to main-
    tain,
With a royal army from Catholic Spain.
Thus kindly encourag'd, the mighty O'Neill
Determined Elizabeth's forces should feel
The might of his pow'r, and the strength of his
    men,
In restoring freedom to Erin again.
John Norris surmising his dangers too great,
Withdrew with his army to avoid defeat
To the town of Armagh, long wedded to fame
In the glories it won through St. Patrick's
    name.
That old honored burrough he took by surprise,
Affecting O'Neill's forces then to despise.
He encamp'd his army before it to show
The Irish could never such strength overthrow.
The chieftain of Tyrone was not unaware

---

† King Philip, of Spain, sent three vessels loaded with powder to O'Donnell and about two hundred men, and promised to aid their cause with men and money. He sent an agent to Ireland to encourage O'Neill and O'Donnell, and assured them of very efficient aid in a short time.

Of the Englishman's strength, and position
　　there,
And fearing to encounter men thus prepared,
Feign'd movements which soon had the Britains
　　ensnared.
The Prince of the North* having marshalled his
　　men,
As if he were anxious the fight to begin;
Then cheering for freedom the soldiers began
To march towards the foe with O'Neill in the
　　van.
His movements were seen by Sir John with a
　　smile,
In which the fierce furies were seen all the
　　while,
As he view'd the approach and gallant display
Of the little army of Ulster that day.
Then looking his own hosts with that conscious
　　pride,
Which makes the vain master his scholars de-
　　ride,

---

* After the English had taken Armagh by surprise, and garrisoned it with a strong force, General Norris encamped his army
convenient to the walls of the city. His position there was too
strong for O'Neill to undertake to lay siege to the place, so he
allured Norris by feigned movements to the Church of Killoter,
where both armies came to an engagement, which resulted in the
utter defeat of the English. The Irish soldiers pursued them under
the very walls of the garrison.

" Those rebels who dared to oppress us of late,
Are now marching onward to a dreadful fate;
Our bright swords shall crimson the sward with
     their gore,
No papist shall live in the land ever more.
Prepare then to meet them my brave gallant
     men,
Rush on to the contest, the battle begin,
We'll teach them to respect our soldiers with
     fear,
They know not their dangers so dreadfully near."
Thus madd'ning his troopers with ire for the
     fray,
He charged on the Irish now flying with dismay;
Their faces agast as if terror was there,
And lent all its fears to the brow of despair;
So real did the feint of their terror appear,
That Norris imagined them stricken with fear;
Then press'd down upon them like the rude
     storms' blast,
When the tempestuous sky 's, with clouds
     overcast.
Thus madly they rushed on the Irishmen's track,

How vain were their efforts, how few should go
    back;
Being led from the walls of the fortified town,
How fearfully dreadful their glory went down;
The clarion voice of the gallant O'Neill
Arose 'bove the din of confusion's loud peal,
As he gave commands to his soldiers to stand,
And wipe out the Saxons from their native land.
The English confused in their headlong career,
Rush'd on to the contest unclouded by fear;
Not knowing the Irish had dared to contend,
When death and destruction they'd meet in the
    end;
Oh! presumptious pride, what delusion is thine,
Thy glories are nursed in the hollow sunshine;
Reflected in dreams, where delusion alone
Imprints all its pow'r in a magical throne.
The Irish had rallied, their flight was a feint,
And Britains proud hosts are all broken and
    bent;
The loud swelling cheers of the North Clans-
    men fall
On the ears of the English, more dreadful than
    all;

They break from their ranks in confusion and
    fright,
And try to escape from their terrors by flight;
But Erin's brave Clans press them back through
    the plain,
Leaving few to return to Armagh again.*
The fame of O'Neill throughout Europe was
    known,
The pride of old Ireland, the star of Tyrone;
From whose brilliant lustre the patriot's fire,
Was lit up through Erin for freedom entire;
That bright ray, so precious, shone gloriously on
Awaking those glories in days that were gone,
When sweet song of freedom, dear Erin were
    thine,
And virtue lent all its pure blessings divine.
His soldiers admired him and honored his name,
His foes paled and trembled when told of his
    fame,
The brave dashing chiefs of his own beloved
    isle,
Grew warm with love in the light of his smile;

---

* After this defeat, Sir John Norris withdrew to Dundalk with
his army, leaving five hundred soldiers behind him to garrison the
city. By this means, O'Neill became master of the field and inter-
cepted whatever provisions were intended for the garrison, so that
famine was the consequence in a short time.

In Connaught,* the old septs gained great renown,

In humbling the forces who fought for the
crown;

Whilst Leinster and Munster still rivaled the
west,

In forcing th' invaders to lie on the dust.

Thus Ireland was roused through the voice of
O'Neill,

To shadow the glow of tyrannical steel,

Which gleam'd through the island in merciless
hands,

Dealing foul destruction through vicious demands.

Old General Norris grew pale with surprise,

And fearing his Queen would forever despise

Her once favored servant, through his sad career,

Withdrew with his army to Dundalk in fear.

He appointed Stafford to the chief command

Of the garrisoned city he'd lately manned;

* O'Donnel having marched with his army to Connaught to aid
the Irish, he laid seige to the Castle of Sligo, which was garrisoned
with two hundred men composed of English and Irish soldiers.
The Irish hearing that their country-men were armed outside, attacked the English, slew the governer (Bingham, the younger) and
surrendered the Castle to O'Donnel, who thereupon appointed
Burke to the Governship thereof. The Castle of Ballimout was
also taken from Bingham, the elder, leaving the condition of the
English in Connaught in a very uncomfortable state.

To guard it with valor 'gainst the papist bands;

Who came to regain it with bold martial hands;

But Hugh of Tyrone and his men held the field,

Determined the Saxons should starve out, or
    yield;

The provisions needed, their wants to supply,

Fell into the Irish, who shouted with joy,

As they bore them away to increase their store,

Leaving the freebooters to suffer the more.

The English in Dundalk, aware of their fate,

And wishing to save them from their wretched
    state,

Equipped a large body, and gave them supplies

To be borne away to Armagh, in disguise;—

How vain was their plotting, how futile their
    plan—

The Irish swept over their ranks to a man.*

---

* After O'Neill had put to the sword the soldiers that had been sent as a guard with a supply of provisions to the English in Armagh, he got some of his men to put on the uniforms of the Britains who had been killed, and ordered them to march to the ruins of a monastry that was within a gun-shot of Armagh. O'Neill then pursued those supposed English with the rest of his men; both parties then began to discharge their muskets, which were loaded with powder only, whereupon the men fell on every side, as instructed. This mock battle within view of the garrison drew the attention of Stafford, who commanded there. He immediately ordered half of his men to repair to the scene of action to aid their countrymen as he supposed, but what was their great surprise when they found those whom they went to aid drawn up in order of battle and ready to charge on them, whilst O'Neill's son lay in ambush with some infantry in the monastry and attacked them in the rear. Being thus placed between two fires they were completely cut to pieces. Stafford seing himself duped acknowledged that he was out-generald and surrendered the garrison to the victorious O'Neill.

Then bearing away all the prizes they 'd won,
Their broad claymores flashing the light of the
    sun;
They hailed their commander with loud Irish
    cheers
And hallowed the greeting with clashing of
    spears.
A bright smile swept o'er his classical face
As he marched back his men with joy to the
    place
Where the hirelings of Bess fell prone to the
    dust,
Surrounded with heroes whose swords felt no
    rust;
Then choosing some men from his brave, fear-
    less clan,
He told them with smiles of his begotten plan.
The clothes of the Britains lying cold on the
    plain
Were donned by the Irish, new glories to gain.
Those troopers were instantly drawn up in line
Their colors shone bright in the mellow sun-
    shine,
Their plumes danced in air as if Queen Bess
    had given

Her soldiers court feathers to fly up to heaven;
In brilliant display they marched proudly on,
Determined the city that day should be won.
O'Neill's dashing forces then charged in their
    rear,
With wild, fearful shoutings, to make it appear
They came with a vengeance to bury their foes
Beneath their fierce onset, with tremendous
    blows;
Then commenced the mock fight, with earnest
    like dread,
Some falling on both sides as if they were dead.
The Irish would soon be the victors, 'twas then
That Stafford addressed his own soldiers
    within—
"Yonder corps, hard pressed, now gloriously
    tries
To bear to this garrison needed supplies;
The Irish have charged on those brave men
    with spite,
They cannot stand longer nor escape by flight,
They waver, they rally, some fall on the plain,
Prepare then to shield them, and avenge their
    slain."

Those curt words of Stafford were cheered loud
    and long,
'Twas the lone wail of death, their said fun'ral
    song.
Then half his doomed soldiers marched out to
    subdue
The impetuous Irish, who dared to pursue
Their heroic brothers, who came to supply
Their wants with provisions when famine was
    nigh;
But, Oh! what dread horrors and wretched
    despair
Knit all their conjectures in war's issues there,
When those who appeared such bold Britains
    before,
Now helped to despatch them, with vengeance
    the more.
The blight of destruction swept over their train,
And all their sad struggles were hushed on the
    plain;
When Stafford beheld his best soldiers cut
    down,
He gave up to O'Neill his claim to the town.
The great Hy Niall chieftain returned his
    thanks

To the dauntless heroes who honored his ranks.
He called them his children, his own valiant
men
Whose glories should honor the old harp again.
Those brave-hearted soldiers regardless of fears,
Stood moved like young women bedew'd with
love's tears;
They blessed him, he loved them, with them he
had toiled,
They cheered him 'till echoes with loud shouts
ran wild,
They entered in triumph the gates of Armagh,
When the British forces were forced to with-
draw,
The joyful inhabitants thronged every street
Where O'Neill was passing, his presence to
greet;
They hailed him as king of his own beloved
isle,
And called him their savior from Britain's laws
vile.
The bashful young maidens before him were
seen
Radiant with joy in their beautiful green;

With white linen handkerchiefs waving in air
Like snow-flakes descending on bosoms as fair.
The mothers with smiles, wedding sweetness
    with grace,
Stood close by their husbands to look at his
    face;
Then silently kissing their young ones with
    love,
They prayed for O'Neill to their Father above.
The old men stood bathed in tears with delight,
When the smiles of the Chief, like Luna's soft
    light,
Passed over their vision as magical bliss—
Enchanting the heart with a fond lover's kiss.
They spoke of his glory, they honored his name,
The Hy Nialls were valiant, distinguished for
    fame;
They gave kings to Ireland before Bryan
    Borough,
That monarch immortal whom none could sub-
    due.
They likened their chief to that hero* of yore,
Whose triumphs were marked by the collar he
    wore.

---

* Malachy, the Monarch of Ireland, 848 A.D.

3

The Cæsar of Erin, their own beloved chief
Who rose to defend them, and banish the thief.
The conquerer rode his white beautiful steed,
Caparisoned over to honor the deed
With trimmings of silver and trappings of gold,
As grand as his fathers in the days of old.
He read on the looks of the old and the young,
Those fond hopes for Erin which lovingly clung
'Round the hearts of her children—faithful and
    true;
Like the ivy matting, the oak with its hue.
His soul was affected with love like their own:
Those fond throbs for Ireland were felt there
    alone,
He knew it, he saw 'twas the bride of his hope,
He loved to embrace it, with it to elope;
To bless his own land with its beauties divine.
The blessings which ever loved freedom are
    thine.
Begotten in Heaven through God's holy will,
It retains its bliss, all its glories until
The power that created its charms alone
Shall bear it from earth to His celestial throne.
He spoke in his love those expressions sublime ·

" Had I, like Joshua, the power to stay time,
I'd show my loved people that Phœbus should
    stand
And shed smiles of freedom all over the land;
The frown of the stranger should pass from our
    shore,
Nor taunt us with mocking delusions no more;
Their haughty presumption should never be-
    night
The glories of Erin with vicious delight.
Your smiles of contentment should playfully
    wed
The brightness of glory which liberty shed,
To help to restore those proud dreams of my
    heart,
I must leave you my friends to perform my
    part."
These last words were wrapt in one continued
    cheer,
Which knit the affections of friendship most
    dear
Between the great chief and his own gallant
    men,
As he led them onward to honor again.

When Stafford imparted to Norris his fate,
He felt that O'Neill was a champion too great
To contend with in arms,—too mindful of fame,
He feared that disgrace might be cast on his
  name,
He instantly ordered his troops to prepare—
His brow overcast with the wrath of despair,
Impressed all his soldiers with silence as deep
As if their expressions were sealed in death's
  sleep.

With thoughts yet of triumph, he set out again
To restore fallen greatness,*in Connaught to win
The honor he lost on the field, through Tyrone,
Yet overshadowing that proud prince alone.
The O'Donnel, soon hearing of his intent,
Called all his brave soldiers around him and went
To meet that bold Britain, who dared to infest
The beauties surrounding the wilds of the West.
Whilst General Norris, with ten thousand men

---

* General Norris, after suffering many serious losses at the
hands of O'Neill in Ulster, determined to gain fresh honors in
place of those he had lost, he accordingly set out for Connaught
with a view of subduing that province. He was joined on his
march by Clanricard, and others, along with having received rein-
forcements from England, his army amounting to about ten thous-
and men ; yet O'Donnel in the vicinity of Ballinroab with five
hundred men, having rejected his terms of peace, forced him to quit
the province after seriously crippling his vast army.

Lay encamped near Athlone, prepared to begin
The contest in Connaught, O'Donnel drew nigh
With five hundred soldiers who seemed to defy
That grand vast array of old troopers who came
To sweep from that province the war plume of
    fame.
Yet all the vauntings of his fierce defiance
Were racked in the throes of his unreliance,
When the chief of Tyrconnel would not disgrace
His own honored name, or the sires of his
    race,
By accepting the peace of the English Queen,
Who tried to dismember old Erin the Green.
Whilst negotiations were daily going on,
O'Donnel's brave rangers great victories won;
At length his disasters caused Norris to fly
From O'Donnel's face, with despair in his eye.
He lost through O'Neill the proud prestage of
    fame,
And gained through Tyrconnel dishonor and
    shame;
Disgraced by his Queen, by Lord Burrough de-
    cried,
Heart-broken, in Munster that old soldier died.

Lord Burrough* was next sent the Irish to
    tame—

He dreamt of the deeds that should honor his
    name;

The rebels should bow down before him like
    slaves,

Or fall, through his pow'r, into premature
    graves;

The old troops of Norris and Russel were sent

To join his own forces, then northwardly bent,

Yet further than Portmor he feared to proceed,

Presentment of dangers had slackened his speed.

Leaving five hundred men to garrison there,

To shoot down the Irish if they should but dare

To intrude their presence, no mercy should save

An Irishman's life who would not be a slave.

Such were the vile wishes of Lord Burrough's
    mind,

The soldiers he left there, as fiercely inclined,

---

* The Queen having recalled deputy Russel in order to re esta-
blish her power once more in Ireland, appointed in his place Lord
Barrough, whose reputation as a military officer was highly flattering. One of his first official acts was in relieving Norris from the
command of the army, and sending him back to the governorship
of Munster forbidding him to leave there without his permission.
The insult weighed heavy on the proud spirit of Norris, he being
already humiliated in his wars with O'Neill. It was supposed that
he died of a broken heart. Burrough was of a fierce and haughty
temperament.

Determined to show him what feats they could
  do
In shooting down papists when they came in
  view;
Their savage intentions were tested at length,
Tirrell, having mustered available strength,
Laid siege to the town with true heroic zeal
To show those base troopers he defied their
  steel.
On his way to Dublin, Lord Burrough was told
That Portmor was threatened with Irishmen
  bold,
He instantly crossed the Blackwater again,
With his colors flying 'bove the ranks of the
  men.
But the gallant chief of Tyrone came that way
And dimmed all his glories of conquest that
  day;
On the road to Benburb the hosts of O'Neill
Stood proudly defiant like statues of steel,
Prepared to resist with the force of their might
The invading Saxons who rushed to the fight,
Like Boreas, sweeping with terrific roar
The forests, as onward it ruthlessly tore.

Lord Burrough commanded his dashing brigade,
Rejoiced in his soul at the show they displayed;
He rushed to the contest, too anxious for blood,
Whilst patiently waiting, the brave Irish stood.
Like the god of battles amidst mortals seen,
O'Neill sat his white steed with grand, lofty
    mien,
In the van, directing the movements of men
Whose glories were never yet equalled since
    then.
Addressing the prince* of the Glynns who
    appeared,
Like a true, noble friend in the vanguard pre-
    pared,
He said: " beloved chieftain, to-day we must
    show
The broad swords of Erin must humble the foe,
The despot shall feel that our mettlesome race
Must never yet bend with the weight of disgrace,
Prepare then to sheathe your broad claymores
    to-day

---

* James McDonnell, Prince of the Glynns, assisted Hugh O'Neill
in the command of his division, whilst his brothers, Cormac and Art
O'Neill, with McMahon, commanded the other division of his army.
Both divisions united in the contest when Burrough endeavored to
force through O'Neill's position.

In hearts long corrupted by tyranny's sway."
The O'Neill remained not to hear the reply—
He read the response in McDonnell's blue eye—
Then hurrying along through the ranks of his
    men,
He cried, "soldiers, forward, to glory again."
One tremendous cheer from those brave clans
    awoke
The lone, silent echoes, which instantly broke
On the peaceful zephyrs like magical dread,
Breathing siren-like wails 'round graves of the
    dead.
Then fearlessly meeting the advancing hosts
Of the men who came to dishonor her coasts,
They fell on their ranks with the sickles of
    death—
The harvest was dreadful, whilst dark terrors
    yet
Grew fearful with action; that day on the plain
Lord Burrough* be'ng wounded could not long
    remain.—
The great Hugh encouraged his men in the van,
His name was the war-cry of each gallant clan;

* Lord Burrough was mortally wounded in the engagement. He
was taken to Newry where he died a few days after.

Unmindful of dangers, no pow'r could with-
    stand
The strength of their love for their unhappy
    land.
Kildare, next in command, the battle renewed
With lioness' fury defending her brood;
But all his skilled efforts were fruitless and void,
He fell in the contest, with his brothers* beside.
The carnage grew dreadful—the groans of the
    dying,
With chargers prancing and lead missiles flying,
Imparted such pictures of horror and fright,
That nature called down from her heights, sable
    night,
To cloak in its bosom of darkness below
The dread scenes of warfare, disorder and woe.
The terrified Britains were stricken with fear,
And fled in dismay like the wild mountain deer
When startled with dread at the cry of the
    hounds,
As if death was inhaled from those awful
    sounds,

---

* The Earl of Kildare, being next in command to Burrough,
renewed the attack with redoubled vigor. but to no avail: he suffered
the same fate as Lord Burrough, dying of his wounds a few days
after the battle. His two foster-brothers were killed by his side in
trying to place him on his horse.

They could not have felt so possessed of des-
    pair
Whilst rushing distractedly from issues there.
The triumphant cheers of the Irish arose,
Proclaiming the utter defeat of their foes.
The victor of Benburb, the great Hugh O'Neill,
Blessed Ireland that day with the clans of the
    Geal.
Those fearful disasters were felt by the crown—
The fame of the army of England went
    down;
Whilst Erin was honored by nations afar,
Her glories shone out from the triumphs of
    war.
The ambitious Ormond* was given command
Of the royal forces, recruited and mann'd;
He felt in his soul the proud herald of fame
Proclaiming the honors surrounding his name.
Determined to prove all his qualities then,
He instantly marched North with eight thou-
    sand men.

* Thomas Duff Butler, Earl of Ormond, was commissioned as Lieutenant-General of Her Majesty's forces in Ireland after the death of Lord Burrough. He was a very ambitious nobleman, who went against his own country for the sake of favor and distinction. He endeavored to bring about a peace with O'Neill, but, after two months' truce hostilities commenced with redoubled action.

Three thousand he ordered against the
　　O'Moore,*
Not doubting a moment that he could endure
The force of such numbers; their destruction
　　fell
On his loyal ears like a funeral bell,
When the dreadful tidings of their wretched
　　state
In sorrowful numbers depicted their fate.

The chieftain of Leix, having strengthened
　　his corps,
Rushed down on the Saxons; the field, which
　　before
Lay smiling in sunshine, now crimsoned with
　　blood,
The tide of life flowing like a dark, swollen
　　flood,
'Till England's paid minions in confusion fled,
And all their proud boastings were hushed as
　　their dead.
Whilst the Britains suffered defeat in the East,

---

* Brian Riaoh O'Murra, or O'Moore, cut to pieces the three
thousand men that were sent against him by Ormond, over one
thousand five hundred of them being slain in battle with their commander. Maryborough was also taken on that occasion by the Irish.

The Marshal's* few triumphs were loudly in-
 creased,
The heralds were praising his glory and worth
In humbling the pride of the Chief of the
 North.
But all their rejoicings were silently nursed
When the pow'r of Bagnal for ever was
 crushed;
The lamp of his glory was quenched in retreat,
And victory's flashes obscured by defeat;
The vain, idle vauntings of envy's foul breath
Were silenced in terror's dark shadows of death,
For Erin's loved hero, impelled by his love
For his native island, registered above
In the High Court of Heaven the vow of his
 heart,
That Bagnal should never from Ireland depart
'Till broken like bent reeds his army should lie,
Where destruction breathes from the sufferer's
 sigh.

---

* The battle of Bealanabuidh took place in the beginning of
August, 1598, near Ardmagh. The battle ground was bound on one
side by a boggy marsh, and on the other by a thick wood. Marshal
Bagnal, with twenty-four of his principal officers and two thousand
of his men, were killed in that dreadful fight. The loss sustained by
O'Neill was about two hundred killed and six hundred wounded.
Twelve thousand pieces of gold, besides arms, provisions of every
kind, and all their artillery, fell into the possession of the Irish, and
the surrender of Portmor.

How fearful he kept his dread promise that day
Was seen in the havoc of death and dismay
Which darken'd with horrors too dreadful for
men
Around the doom'd ranks of those freebooters
then.
Had Jupiter hurled his thunderbolts dread
From high-topped Olympus, the great fountain
head
Of the immortal gods, they could not affright
Elizabeth's troopers like that dreadful fight.
They broke from their ranks in confusion, and
fled
From the field of battle, strewn with their dead.
The victor of Benburb was honor'd once more
As the great defender of his native shore.
The crushed cause of freedom in Munster arose
Through the triumphs gained by O'Neill from
his foes;
The chiefs* of that province determined to stand

---

* Fitzmaurice, Fitzgerald, the Knight of Kerry, Fitzgerald,
Knight of the Glynn and Edmond Fitzgerald, called the "White
Knight," together with Dermod and Donogh McCarty, and several
other chieftains, once more formed a league against the Queen. The
bravery of the renowned Earl of Desmond, whose deeds left an ever-
lasting testimony of fame and love behind him, filled their hearts
with heroism. They appointed James Fitzgerald, surnamed the
"Red," as their leader, and acknowledged him as Earl of Desmond.
The Prince of Tyrone aided them with men and money in their
glorious struggle.

Once more for the rights of their own native land.
They wrote to the bountiful Prince of Tyrone
To aid their exertions with troops of his own;
He blessed their endeavors with greetings of joy,
And sent them his brother with men who would
    die
To humble the pow'r of the Queen on that soil
Where Desmond's blood flow'd in defense of
    the isle.
The proud loyal Ormond still held the command,
Yet all his ambition for fame in the land
Was damp'd by the great chief, who manfully
    'rose
With lion-like courage and conquer'd his foes.
Her majesty, fearful of losing her claim
In Ireland, sent over a young man* of fame,
With a pow'rful army, prepar'd and equipp'd,
Determin'd O'Neill's forces then should be
    whipp'd—
Yet Ireland's brave heroes undaunted remained,
Their swords still unsheathed whilst British
    blood stained

---

* Robert d'Evereaux, Earl of Essex, landed in Ireland on the 15th day of April, 1599. The Queen invested him with extraordinary power and provided him with an army of seventeen thousand foot and thirteen hundred horse, the largest force that had yet been sent to Ireland.

Their fields with its dark hue, which fearfully told
What Erin had done for her freedom of old.
The landing of Essex to conquer O'Neill,
Became the great cry through the land of the
     Gael ;—
The Englishmen lauded their hero alone,
Whilst the Irish claim'd for the Prince of
     Tyrone,
That no foreign soldier could ever destroy
The strength of his might, or the flash of his eye ;
The immortal gods dare not themselves offend
A chieftain so valiant, as their Ulster friend.
Thus conflicting comments were rumored about,
'Till Essex for Munster with his corps set out,
Resolved to subdue that old province at first
And humble the pride of its chiefs to the dust,
But there he encountered the McCarty More*
And Desmond, whose forces triumphantly bore
The laurels of fame they so glor'ously won
From England's proud Earl, her own beloved
     son.

---

* Daniel McCarty More and the Earl of Desmond, with an army of about two thousand five hundred men, encountered Essex at a place called Baile-en-Firntere, on his way back from Askeaton. The English outnumbered the Irish about three to one, yet the battle lasted from 9 o'clock in the morning till five o'clock in the afternoon. The English loss was dreadful whilst the valiant sons of Ireland had escaped the bloody contest with a far lighter number slain.

When the ambitious hopes of the Earl went
 down
In Munster's broad lands, for the cause of the
 crown,
He wrote off to Clifford, to join without fail
His army in Ulster, to crush the O'Neill;
But Tyrconnel's chieftain† disputed his way,
Their armies encounter'd about Lady's Day;
The governor fell on the red field of war,
Whilst all who escap'd death were scatter'd afar.
The proud soul of Essex was shrouded with
 grief,
When the men he looked for to give him relief
Were crush'd in their march by O'Donnel the
 brave,
And Clifford, the tyrant, sent down to the grave,
Where dark winding shadows of grim terrors
 led
To dread yawning depths of Plutonian dead.

---

† The O'Donnel came to an engagement with Clifford, on his way
to Ulster, where he intended to join the army of the Earl of Essex,
according to the instructions given him by the latter. The battle took
place at the pass of the Corslieve Mountain, and was maintained with
great vigor by both parties with like success until the gallant O'Rourke
at the head of a body of infantry, appeared on the scene of action
and turned the scale of victory on the side of the Irish. Clifford was
killed in the engagement with fourteen hundred of his men. The
total number that fell on the side of the Irish was one hundred and
forty men. The Earl of Essex was greatly discouraged by the defeat
of the governor of Connaught and his army.

4

Fresh troopers from England were order'd
    once more
To increase the thinn'd ranks of the new Earl's
    corps;
But when he march'd forward to meet the great
    Prince,
His soldiers committed a cowardly offense.*
Like aspen leaves shaken by the storm's blast,
When dark, murky clouds heaven's arch over-
    cast,
They trembled and pal'd when O'Neill came in
    view
With his lov'd brigade, ever faithful and true.
Poor Essex beheld them with sorrowful eyes,
To lead them to battle thus, would be unwise;
He knew what the soldier of Benburb could do;
Disasters would darken around him anew,
Should he dare contend with the Prince of
    Tyrone,
That hero whose fame throughout Europe was
    known.
He wisely refrained from the contest that day,

---

* Lombard says, when the English saw the Irish so well prepared, and eager for the engagement, they were so panic-struck that
they were covered with shame, and afraid to hold up their heads.

And school'd his ambition with thoughtful
delay,
By humbly requesting O'Neill to accede*
To a truce of six weeks, to which he agreed;
Then spending some time with the chief, he set
out
For Dublin, dejected and weary, no doubt,
Evolving the issues of trouble and care,
Which shrouded his hopes in the gloom of
despair.
He thought of the glory surrounding his name,
The love of his Queen, when to Ireland he came,
The army which followed his standard alone,
Was all he could wish to gain conquests un-
known.
Yet all his career in the land of the green,
Was ruin and disaster to him, and his Queen;
He felt that his glory must now pass away

---

*The Earl of Essex, seeing the cowardly condition of his soldiers,
sent a herald to O'Neill declaring that he came not as an enemy into
his province, but to offer him terms of peace, and that he would
send commissioners to confer with him in the matter, if the Prince
would accede to his request. The terms proposed by the commissioners were rejected by O'Neill. Essex then sent his army to Drogheda, and went himself to the camp of the Irish chieftain, accompanied by a few nobles. The two soldiers having met, Essex be-
sought the Prince to feel some sympathy for the humbled position of
the son of his former friend (O'Neill and the Earl's father were two
friends.) The great heart of O'Neill could not resist such an appeal.
He accordingly granted him six weeks' truce. The time being settled,
the two spent some time together in social enjoyment.

When ordered to England without much delay,

Before that his truce with O'Neill had expir'd,

Which wounded his proud soul for thus being
    retir'd.*

When Philip† the Third had ascended the
    throne,

He wish'd to encourage the Prince of Tyrone

In his war with the Queen; he 'cordingly sent

Him a royal present to prove his intent.

Encourag'd and hoping for greater success

From the Spanish monarch, to humble Queen
    " Bess."

The notice‡ requir'd by the truce to be giv'n,

Was sent to Mountjoy‖ on a bright starry even;

His Lordship assum'd to make peace§ with the
    Prince;

* Elizabeth greatly reproached the Earl of Essex for his contempt of her commands, and had him recalled from Ireland about the middle of September, A. D. 1600.

† When Philip the Third succeeded his brother as King of Spain he sent two legates to Ireland with a crown of phœnix feathers, twenty-two thousand pieces of gold and some kegs of silver, to the Prince of Ulster, besides giving him every assurance of speedy assistance.

‡ According to the truce agreed between O'Neill and Essex, a notice of fourteen days should be given by whichsoever party wished to commence hostilities first.

‖ Charles Blunt, Baron of Mountjoy, was appointed Viceroy after the recall of Essex, and at the same time Sir George Carew was given the Presidency of Munster.

§ Mountjoy tried to induce O'Neill to give up the war in Ireland by offering him the free exercise of his religion and reparation for the injuries sustained by the Catholics. But the Prince knew their promises too well, and could not be influenced by the deputy to accede to any doubtful terms.

But all his assumption and grand eloquence
Were lost to that chieftain; he knew that the
    word
Of England with foul shame and sorrow was
    blur'd.
Her promises never were faithfully kept,
For dark deeds, like shadows of grim evils crept
Where innocence slept in the hope of her trust,
And realized only polluted disgust.
The Viceroy, enrag'd at the tone of the chief,
Determin'd to bring him to sorrow and grief;
He 'cordingly hasten'd his army along,
Like the " King of Men," in Homerian song;
He sent a large fleet to a lake, called Loughfoyle,
The soldiers commenced a grand forage in style,
About fifteen hundred were met by O'Neill,
Who dreadfully felt the great force of his steel;
Their shades hover'd over that dread field of woe
Where death and disorder slept shrouded below.
Mountjoy grew amaz'd at the great slaughter
    there,
And order'd his forces forthwith to prepare
To march back to Dublin, they could not with-
    stand

Those fearless Milesians who fought for their
    land;
Yet, Erin's exertions, unaided, alone,
Though sway'd by the god-like, the mighty
    Tyrone,
Could never regain her long-lost liberty,
Without a strong fleet to protect her at sea.
Her harbors lay spaciously open all 'round,
Denuded of forces, her foes to astound;
Whilst England's fleet rode on the waves of her
    shore,
Belching forth iron-hail from the cannon's bore,
And bearing recruits like wild savages shorn
Of human reflections, degraded, forlorn,
To harrow the peace of her innocent soul,
With crimes sanctioned only by demons' control.
Yet fearlessly hoping, the great Irish chief,
Determined to stand out, 'till Spanish relief
Could aid him to expel the hordes of the Queen
From the land of his sires, whose glories were
    seen
In grand, royal pomp and pageant of yore,
Which hallow'd the monarchs of the Shamrock
    shore.

Mountjoy having strengthen'd his army again,
And meeting with Lambert and his wicked men,
Wherever those tyrants went forth without fear
Destruction denoted their hellish career;
At length they agreed that their forces should
    try,
The chieftain who seemed British pow'r to defy,
If Mountjoy could conquer that great hero now,
New laurels of fame would adorn his brow;
He'd gain the reward,* and his glory alone
Should eclipse forever the Mars of Tyrone.
To the North the armies were hasten'd along,
Their fame should be heard of in story and song;
They nursed the delusion with delusive joy,
'Till the Prince of Ulster with his men drew
    nigh;
Fears, doubts, hopes and terrors of what might
    arise,
Were felt in their hearts, were seen in their
    eyes.
They dared not encounter, yet feared to retreat,
Disgrace and contempt would be worse than
    defeat;

---

* A proclamation about this time was issued by the English government, offering a reward of two thousand pounds to any party who would deliver O'Neill into their hands alive, or one thousand pounds for his head.

For two weeks they kept within sight of 'ONeill,
The bright sun of August shone down on their
    steel,
Imparting the sheen of their brilliant display
To the sons of Erin, in martial array.
Determin'd at length, with one desperate aim,
To unman the Irish, with chivalrous fame
They rushed with the fury of demons prepared
To cut down the Irish; no one should be saved;
But the sons of Ireland, as fearless and brave
As lions watching ov'r their young in some cave,
Resisted the shock of the advancing foe
With crushing resistance, which laid thousands
    low.
The war-clouds arose with deep, shadowing
    gloom,
And smoked the surroundings from the cannon's
    boom;
Whilst clashing of sabres rang loud on the ear,
With mingled commotions of horror and fear;
The tramping of horses in confusion rose,
Impressing the gods with the conflict of foes,
Whilst doleful expressions of death-rending
    cries,

In wild exclamations, arose to the skies.

The gods seemed to move in their dread issues
    there,

As the British hosts broke their ranks in
    despair;

Four thousand* lay stretch'd on the empurpl'd
    plain—

The brave sons of Erin had triumph'd again;—

Their cheers, their rejoicings were greetings of
    love,

To the God of battles, all glorious above;—

And their own belov'd Prince, the immortal
    Hugh,

Whose glories shall ever shine brilliant and new,

He stood by to guide them, to win back their
    own

From the polluted grasp of the British throne.

The dark persecutions of religious spleen,

Which Ireland had suffered through the English
    Queen,

---

* Mountjoy marched, in October, A. D. 1600, for Ulster, at the head of six thousand men. He did not proceed far when he met with the O'Neill. The two armies continued in sight of each other fifteen days without attempting anything, after which two battles were fought— one near Dundalk and the other near Carlingford. The English lost upwards of four thousand men; the deputy was dangerously wounded and carried away to Newry to be cured. (See Mooney's History of Ireland, page 686.)

Impress'd in the heart of that hero of fame,
That Erin should try to recover her name;—
In matchless encounters his valor was tried;
He harrow'd the foeman like foam on the tide,
When swept by the blast of some terrific gale,
Or crush'd by the force of some fast-sweeping
    sail.
To bless the great chieftain, with pleasure and
    pride,
The youths and the maidens oft knelt by his
    side;
Their innocence sway'd, affected his soul,
With tender emotions he could not control:
He labor'd to save them from every disgrace
Whilst England had tried to wipe out the old
    race;
His efforts triumphantly, glor'ously rose,
Like the great Archangel, subdu'ng Heaven's
    foes.
They fear'd the proud crest of the mighty Tyrone
As dreamers oppres'd by grim terrors unknown;
Though his ranks were reduced by the storms
    of war,
He stood forth alone, like that beautiful star,

Awaiting the rise of bright Phœbus at morn,
When golden reflections the high hills adorn;
He thought of his own belov'd, beautiful land,
When virtue and glory walked forth hand in
    hand,
Like Heaven-born sisters, divinely impress'd
With the scenes 'round the loveliest land of the
    West.
Then, sadly reflecting, he gazed on her woes,
Her sorrows increased with the pow'r of her
    foes;
He drew his broad claymore to stay their
    career,
And the flash of its sheen had 'waken'd their
    fear.
They trembled before him like serfs of the land
When the " Red-Hand " wav'd o'er his own
    gallant band;
But continued war had diminished his men,
Whilst fresh Britains landed, and increased
    again
The ranks of the foes he had thinn'd in his
    might,
Like Hector of yore in the great Trojan fight.

And like that brave soldier, when guarding his
 Troy

From Grecians who came its proud walls to
 destroy,

He battled more God-like, when nought but
 despair

Like grim shadows trembled, and seem'd to
 declare

" The hopes of thy country are passing away;

The Spaniards have failed to fulfill what they
 say,

The South* is subdued, and thy glories alone

Cannot vanquish thousands,† Oh! mighty
 Tyrone."

Yet dared he, and fought still the armies of
 " Bess,"

Rely'ng on the promise of the King's address—

But that look'd for succor when rumored at
 length,

To have left Spain for Erin, was shorn of
 strength—

---

* Carew, the President of Munster, having in the month of July,
A.D. 1600, destroyed the growing crops, and burned what was already
harvested, caused a dreadful famine, which swept away thousands
of the Irish, and made that province an easy conquest, with the ex-
ception of the army of the Earl of Desmond, which amounted to
about six hundred men, who still kept up some show of resistance.

† The English were constantly receiving re-enforcements from
their own land, whilst the Irish thus far received no aid from abroad

The fates had decreed that the wild tempest
    blast
Should scatter the fleet, when its white sails at
    last
Like aerial messengers, were seen to move
O'er vastness of waters impell'd by their love.
Don Juan, with a part of his shattered sail,
Arrived in the harbor of ancient Kinsale;
The Irish threw open the gates of the town,
And flocked to his standard, to fight for their
    own.
Mountjoy, with an army of eight thousand men,
Surrounded the place to confine them therein;
Whilst Levison's fleet in the harbor pour'd
    down
Destructive red-shot to demolish the town.
Yet fearlessly braving the pow'r of the foe,
Those brave, gallant soldiers dealt many a blow
To the haughty foeman with crushing dismay,
Which harrow'd the soul of the tyrant each
    day—
The princes, O'Neill and O'Donnel, set out
From their Northern homes for the land of the
    South,

To effect a concerted action with Don,
That Erin's bright name might live glor'ously
    on.
The English, sixteen thousand strong, well
    prepared,
Encountered their forces, who fearlessly dared
To oppose such numbers, yet bravely they
    stood
'Till their foes were drench'd with the embat-
    tled flood—
The terrible odds of the English at length
Swept over the Irish and master'd their
    strength;
The expected Spaniards* came not to their aid
'Till hundreds were slain of the Irish Brigade.
O'Neill seeing his best men cut down in his
    sight,
By three times their numbers contending in
    fight,
Withdrew from the contest his brave men, with
    care,

* A concerted action having been agreed upon by the O'Neill and Don Juan, the Irish were full of sanguine hopes and attacked an army over three times their numbers, relying on the aid of the Spaniards, but their commander did not lead his troops out of the garrison until it was too late, consequently the Irish were defeated, and O'Neill lost in that engagement about twelve hundred men.

Whilst Englishmen rushed wild to slaughter
    them there.

He march'd back to Ulster with his colors fly-
    ing,

His looks yet determin'd, as if still defying

The baseless usurper who came to destroy

The peace of his country, her beauty and joy.

O'Donnel embark'd for the Old land of Spain,

To try to raise forces for Ireland again;

A new fleet was ready with that Prince to sail,

When Don Juan* surrendered the Town of
    Kinsale.

The lonely glen echoes from silence awoke,

Like the thunders' loud peals, which instantly
    broke

O'er high-peaked Olympus, to stop the career

Of Tytans disdaining the great Jove to fear.

The wild cry of treason was all that was heard,

The echoes distinctly repeated that word;

---

* Don Juan del Aquila, the commander of the Spanish fleet, surrendered the town of Kinsale to the English when all their stores
were nearly out. According to many historians they were completely
exhausted, and their provisions were not sufficient to last six days
longer, while Don Juan was well provided with ammunition and provisions. The garrison was well manned with two thousand five hundred men. There were grave suspicions entertained against the
commander of the garrison in consequence of this uncalled-for surrender. All foreign aid, by this dishonorable act of his, was shut out
from Ireland.

Don Juan had betray'd his trust to the foe,

The freedom of Erin was stunn'd by the blow.

The province of Munster was all but subdued,

When the chieftain of Barre* the contest
     renewed;

His castles alone were yet his to retain,

They were not disgraced by that false son of
     Spain.

Dunboy, with its matchless heroes, alone

Gave proof of such valor, no mortals have
     shown;

Their glories shall ever resplendently shine

'Round th' alter of fame, at the patriot's shrine.

The lion of the North, the shield of his land,

The glory of Erin with his gallant band,

Though humble in numbers, still terror in-
     spired

In the foeman's heart through the fame they
     acquired.

For years he had humbled the insolent Queen,

Whose social connection with Erin had been

---

* O'Sulleven Bearre, feeling uneasy at the conduct of Don Juan, took possession of the Castle of Dunboy, which belonged to him, but which he had given to the Spaniards as a garrison when they first landed. He wrote a letter to the King of Spain explaining his motives, and at the same time criticised the action of Don Juan as wretched, inhuman and execrable.

A disgraceful effort in trying to subdue
A race more exalted than she ever knew.
Her frenzied career overshadowed the Isle
With dread persecutions, which made men
    recoil
From horrors too dreadful for nature to bear,
In trying to proclaim herself as priestess there.
Yet all her exertions were fruitless and vain,
The Papal Tiara she could not obtain;
All England might bow at her fanciful shrine,
But Irishmen never could think her divine.
For years, the great O'Neill had battled for
    right,
The fame of her soldiers went down in his sight;
She tried to ensnare him by bribes and decrees,
The Red-Hand flung proudly its folds to the
    breeze;
The daughter of Ann Boleyn could not tear
    down
The banner of Ulster, though wearing a crown.
Th' invincible soldier, the prince of Tyrone,
Whose immortal glory shall ever be known,
So humbled the tyrantess that she decreed
She could not become head of the Irish creed.

5

Whatever concessions O'Neill* had required,
Were instantly granted as soon as desired;
Thus peace was restored to the land of the
     Gael,
And blessings decked fame 'round the brow of
     O'Neill.

----

    * The terms of peace offered to O'Neill were a general amnesty for himself and his allies, a free exercise of their religion, and the peaceful enjoyment of their estates. Thus the great O'Neill with his gallant little army of a mere handful, compared to the superior numbers of his enemies, after fifteen years war, forced England to yield to his demands.

IRISH NATIONAL EFFUSIONS.

ERIN'S SOUL OF FREEDOM.

The soul of freedom, Erin mine,
From thy green shores has fled—
The beauties of thy ancient bow'rs
Which peaceful sweetness shed.
No more can hallow scenes as fair,
The despot's dreaded frown
Has stained the pride of glories there,
And wears a bloody crown.

The glories of the past, which told
Of Erin's pow'r and name,
Are hid within the graves of old—
Of heroes known to fame;
But from their memories, nursed within
The hearts of Erin's own—
Love, valor, wit, shall bless again
That land where they were known.

COERCION LAWS IN IRELAND.

A land submerged in sorrow's tears,
An island crushed by tyrants' sway,
Arises from surrounding fears
Like sunshine chasing shades away.
The dark impending gloom which hung
Around its peaceful zenith, cast
A pall of wretched woes among
A people's love, too grand to blast.

The nation felt the spreading gloom
Which hemmed her in on every side;
Her beauties which were want to bloom,
Had faded from the land and died.
The merry laugh which filled the plain,
And music'd every grove and bow'r,
Is stilled within that sad domain—
Hushed by the tyrant's damning pow'r.

The land which freedom gave to song,
When peace and plenty crown'd her brow

In famine's dread distress too long,
Though British rule was crushed 'till now.
When overburdened woes pressed on,
And graver threats than mocking woe
Swept all the glories she had won,
She donned herself to meet the foe.

Her armor was the sage's lore,
Her sword, the pen which told to men
The wrongs for which she bled before,
And dared to stand and bleed again.
On every mountain, glen and vale,
Her people met to change her laws,
The land-lords, in their efforts fail
To meet the issues—union draws.

The gover'mental gory-head
With gaping jaws of belching ire,
Too long with ghastly horrors fed,
Arises from its bloody mire.
This monster grim with fiendish frown,
Not satiated yet with gore,
Another code of laws lays down,
To shoot Old Ireland's sons once more.

For this coercion has been passed
Through it the butcheries wrought each hour,
Were nursed with its foul deadly blast,
The hatch-plot of a minion's pow'r.
The upstart's wish becomes a law,
A bloody spectre mounts the throne;
Grim horrors feed upon, and draw
The principles which God had sown.

CHICAGO'S WELCOME TO PARNELL.

On the occasion of his Visit to Chicago, February, 1879.

Welcome Parnell, Chicago bids thee welcome
With throbbing hearts, which swell
With greetings none can tell;
Sublimely reaching out to thee, Parnell.

All hail, immortal son of fame,
Chicago greets thy honor'd name
With drums and trumpets swelling loud,
And thousands sway'ng, the rushing crowd
All anxious to extend to thee
A nation's blessings, grand and free.

From out the dark surroundings grave,
Which shrouds thy native land
With gloomy shadows like some cave,
Which death and dismal horrors manned;
Thy name untarnish'd bursts the gloom,
The farmers' sad hearts to illume.

Too long the vanities of pride
Have nursed degenerate laws,
And sunk beneath corruption's tide
Old Ireland's long-lost cause;
But yet that pride of freedom's right,
Within true souls lives on
Until that right shall conquer might,
And bless new glories won.

To proud Columbia's happy shore,
Where freedom's sunshines smile,
We greet thee, and thy friend* once more,
Loved sons of Erin's Isle.
The garden city of the West,
With thund'ring plaudits, tell
The joys arising from her breast,
To welcome thee, Parnell.

---

* John Dillon, M.P.

THOUGH SHADOWED THE GLORIES.

Though shadow'd the glories which mirror'd
    thy freedom
When liberty's echoes awakened thy name,
And hallow'd thy beauty with sweetness which
    seldom
Transcendently lights up the nations of fame;
Though dim be the ray, mellow'd yet by that
    glory
Which sanctified freedom and sweet liberty,
Its light shall still brighten the pages of story
Which love has embosomed dear Erin in thee.

Though vile bloody vampires have drank at the
    fountain
Of richness of freedom so truly thine own,
Until the bright sun shine which kisses each
    mountain
Is clouded with dark dreaded horrors unknown;
Yet proudly we love thee though long bitter
    sorrow
Hangs over thy bosom, my dear native isle,
The frown of the foeman can never yet shadow
The sweetness of love in true liberty's smile.

THE IRISH VOLUNTEERS.

Remember the days of the brave volunteers,
Whose glories reflected the fame of their sires,
Like true-hearted soldiers regardless of fears
They illum'd the nation with liberty's fires;
The sheen of their armor o'er mountain and
    dale
Shed lustre as bright as the beams of the sun,
And fill'd the large hearts of the sons of the
    Gael
With fame, which their fathers so often had
    won.

The British usurper beheld with dismay
The fame-crested heroes of Erin's green shore,
And fearing their prowess in martial array
Acceded to wishes denied oft before;
The national rights of old Ireland once more
Inspired the proud souls of the brave volunteers
Uniting their forces in one army corps,
The glens of green Erin were fill'd with their
    cheers.

Demosthenes like in defence of their land,
The iron-voiced Grattan led on by their tone,
The spirit of freedom with eloquence fann'd,
'Till England declar'd her a nation alone;
Oh, Erin! what proud happy days were then
    thine,
Thy free trade restor'd and thy children 'gain
    free,
The belching artill'ry, thy freedom divine,
Flash'd to other nations far over the sea.

Such happy days are they faded for ever,
It is treason to wish their return again,
But vain 's the tyrant who trys to dissever
Affections so holy, so glor'ous as then.
Those brave volunteers are uniting once more,
The spirit of Emmet inspires them to fame,
The freedom and virtue of the Shamrock shore
Shall burst from the fetters of England's foul
    shame.

SHALL THE HOPES OF ERIN, &c.

Shall the hopes of Erin which link our affections
To Erin enthron'd on the waves of the deep,
Remain like a dreamer's somnif'rous reflections,
Which are but the fanciful pictures of sleep.

Unknown'd shall we live in the throes of sub-
    jection,
Cold, cold and unhonor'd our names to remain,
No halo of glory shall throw its reflection
O'er graves which the essence of cowardice
    would stain.

Shall the steel of the foeman contempt'ously
    gleam
In the heart of a nation to terrors unknown,
When chivalrous warriors have power to re-
    deem
That land from the tyrant unaided, alone.

The coward and the slave shall be ever united,
No glory awaits them, in bondage they're led,
The heart of the soldier is always delighted
With the rays of freedom his sabre has shed.

Gird on then your arms, let your glories awaken
The echoes of fame which surrounded your
    sires,
Go, teach the usurper old Ireland's unshaken,
Her battle for liberty never expires.

THE HEROINES OF LIMERICK.

Beneath the dark continued smoke,
Which overcast the peaceful sky,
As when death flung his dismal cloak
Around the ancient walls of Troy,
The women of Old Limerick town,
Gained for themselves love and renown.

When the strong walls were batter'd down
By the dread missiles of the foe,
And whilst the cannon's angry frown
Imparted terrors wild and woe,
Those heroines rush'd to the breach
Like billows leaping to the beach.

With their brave brothers side by side,
Their fathers and their sons they stood
Regardless of the swelling tide,
Grow'ng fiercer in the battle's flood;
With weapons taken from the slain,
Their country's rights they did maintain.

Within the hollow of death's pale,
They fought to conquer or to die,
And stood before the iron hail
Until the foeman had to fly;
Oh! brave immortal women true,
Your country shall remember you.

THE LAND I LOVE SO WELL.

There is an island sweetly ly'ng within the
    ocean's breast,
Where beauty suns its ancient bow'rs with
    magic charms blest;
Where fragrance fills the perfumed air with
    flow'rs from every dell,—
That island is my Irish home, the land I love
    so well.

Surrounded by the breakers wild from the
    Atlantic deep,
It rises like an angel fair from surging mystic
    sleep,—
The sweetness of its purity from nature seems
    to swell,—
That island is my Irish home, the land I love
    so well.

The youth of virgin's modesty is felt within its
    clime,
Its ancient language mellow'd with the beauti-
    ful, sublime;
From innocence its children sip the virtues
    which dwell
Within my native Irish home, that land I love
    so well.

Its fields are green with verdant hue, the birds
    from every bow'r
Carol their matin songs of love to wed the
    fleeting hour
To charms nursed by grace divine, too sweet
    for man to tell,—
Within my own loved island home, that land I
    love so well.

The pure rippling streams indenting its surface
    like the veins
Which course the human body through, supply
    it greater means
To irrigate her fruitful soil with beauties, which
    excell,
Throughout my native Irish land, that land I
    love so well.

Yet from that land estrang'd, unknown, I'm
    forced from her to stray,
The tyrant's chains surround her now, until
    they're cut away
By martial Irish valor, whose deeds of fame
    shall tell—
That Ireland is proud freedom's home; dear
    land, farewell, farewell!

IF IRELAND WOULD BE FREE.

If Ireland would be free
From British Tyranny,
The soul of strength alone,
• Like God's love 'round His throne,
Must fill the heart and nerve the hand
To bear triumphant war's demand.

In union, men possess
The greatness which impress
The force and pow'r of might
When nations spring to light,
From glories signalized in war,
When bless'd by union's guiding star.

Distrust imprisons pow'r,
When freedom's golden hour
Invites the heroe's fame
Her love, her joys to claim;
Ah! love divine, distrust destroys
Thy virgin soul where glory lies.

If Ireland would be free,
Then let true unity
Impress its love within
The hearts of Irishmen,
Then Erin's fame shall show its light
'Round freedom's altar day and night.

THE MEETING OF THE CLANS.

DEDICATED TO THE IRISH AMERICANS.

Sons of Ireland's chivalry, true sons of sires ot
fame,
The silence of the martyrs graves, those graves
of British shame
Which lie neglected in the land, that land for
which they died,
Demands the union of the clans, those men of
Erin's pride;
The stalwart, brave, united sons, of sons who
dared to show
Their fathers were true Irishmen, can yet repel
the foe.

The spirit of submission to the freebooters'
    laws,
Was never nurs'd with the heart of freedom's
    holy cause;
That cause is Ireland's burning love, for that
    her martyrs fall,
Unite clans at our country's wail, responsive to
    her call;
The day of union marks the dawn of Ireland's
    liberty,
Through hearts united in her fame she can be
    ever free.

What though the weight of centuries of in-
    juries and woe
Is heaped upon our gallant race, by an ungrate-
    ful foe,
The brighter should the lamp of hope in every
    true heart burn,
'Till England's power was made to feel our
    power in return;
Such power in union centers, and dreaded
    issues spans,
Let union be your link of hope, brave, fearless
    Irish clans.

WHY IRELAND SHOULD BE FREE.

Why Ireland should be free,
Was question'd once of me;—
The stranger knew not why
That Irishmen should cry,
Expel those English hordes;
Proclaim it through the chords
Of Tara's Harp, which fame
Awoke to sing the name
Of *one whose brilliant glories gave
True love, to wed a soldier's grave.

Go, read her deeds, I said,
See how her children bled;—
The story of her wrongs
Lives in her bardic songs.
The hireling treachery
Of English perfidy
Ne'er can be wip'd away
Whilst British laws there sway;
An Irishman can't live a slave—
He'd rather fill a soldier's grave.

* Brian Borough.

Our commerce they've destroy'd,
Our glories they've belied
And filled the land with woes—
Like bestial, savage foes,
The innocent, the young,
On their barb'd steel they flung.—
Ask if we can forget
Such deeds, Oh! never yet,
Whilst God in mercy spares our race,
No despot shall our land disgrace.

MY FRIENDS ACROSS THE SEA.

'Tis sweet to think of days gone by, when
    friendship's love divine
Stole softly o'er my youthful soul, when pleas-
    ures wild were mine,
When fortune show'r'd her golden hours
    around my friends and me,
Before I dreamt of foreign lands, or thought to
    cross the sea.

What kindness nursed my little heart and fed
    my tender mind,
When friends imparted blessings, those friends
    I left behind,
When sun-shine smiles of happiness were all
    that I could see
Within the bosom of my own, my friends across
    the sea.

But all these happy days are changed, no
    parents greet me now,

The toiling weight of passing years leans heavy
    on my brow,
Those childish ways I loved of yore before my
    vision flee,
Since I withdrew in sorrow from my friends
    across the sea.

A mother's burning love no more can cheer her
    lonely son,
Within the grave she molders now — her mor-
    tal course is run,
Her generous counsels are shut off by stern
    death's decree,
She sleeps the silent sleep of death away
    beyond the sea.

My father too is lost to me, his voice I hear no
    more,
Although he battles bravely on through life's
    stream at four-score,
But how I miss his soft sweet smile, that smile
    I lov'd to see
Before I left my native home to cross the
    stormy sea.

And often in my lonely walks, my sisters, kind
and true,
My thoughts recall those happy days when I
had walked with you,
And listened to the songs you sung so sweet
beneath yon tree,
Which overtopped our country cot, beyond the
rolling sea.

And, Oh! what sorrows cloud my mind when
I enjoy no more,
The companionship of brothers with whom I
wander'd o'er
The rolling valleys clothed with flowers for the
honey bee,
Which grew spontaneous in that land, my home
across the sea.

To the despoilers of my land I could not bow
the knee,
I cross'd the stormy ocean, determined to be
free,
Beneath the " Starry Banner" my future home
shall be,
But yet my heart belongs to you, dear friends
across the sea.

TO THE IRISH–AMERICAN SOCIETIES.

Expatriated heroes, undaunted sons of fame—
Untarnished by dishonor,
Lovers of the " Starry Banner,"
The land of saints and sages, a mother's rights
    still claim.

Oppress'd by foreign despots who mock her
    ancient lore,
And introduce with nervous haste
New Saxon laws, base and unchaste,
Where justice held her balance pois'd with
    confidence before.

From the surging ocean's billows she lifts her
    head to thee—
As mother she has nursed you well,
Although the tyrants horrors swell
Within her soul, unblemished, save by her
    enemy.

On you she calls as children to lead her as of
   yore,
From the foul depths of oppression,
When the Northmen held possession,
And barbarously revelled in shedding human
   gore.

Remember England's treachery, the pledges
   she broke,
Her shameless acts through ages long
Recorded oft in prose and song,
And with united effort, strike off the foreign
   yoke.

In union there is strength and love, then let
   that union be
The stepping stone to freedom's land,
Where heroes linking hand in hand,
Stand bravely for one holy cause, the cause of
   liberty.

ARISE FOR FREEDOMS CAUSE.

Arise! arise St. Patrick's sons, arise for free-
    doms cause,
And gird the sword of valor on, lest former
    fame withdraws;
Never would your sires of yore bow down in
    slav'ry,
Whilst there remain'd one native spark to con-
    sume tyranny.

Your former rights are buried in the graves
    where now repose
The silent ashes of your sires, crush'd down
    by foreign foes,
Engraft their fame within your hearts and
    resurrect their rights,
The angels 'round the croppies' graves shall
    guard you in your plights.

Why linger on the slave's domain, where
    tyranny has said:

Bind on those chains you abject race, before me
    bow the head,
Subject yourselves as menials, and worship at
    my shrine,
My will is law, my word supreme, your life,
    your all, is mine.

No descendant of Miletius who loves his native
    shore,
Can calmly fold his hands in peace, and wish to
    wield no more
The glitt'ring sword which patriots triumph-
    antly uphold
As emblems of their country's love, far dearer
    than pure gold.

Arise! arise! then Irish sons, and stay the
    tyrant's might
Which lingers in your native land, to sow dis-
    cord and blight;
Unfold your own lov'd flag once more, o'er
    Tara's ancient hall,   .
And British pow'r shall soon become another
    Danish fall.

LORD CASTLEREAGH.

[Supporting the Legislative Union Bill in the Irish House of Parliament.]

Oh! Castlereagh, false Castlereagh!
How sad, how cheerless was the day,
When, for the sake of British pelf,
You sold your country and yourself,
And let the tyrant loose once more,
To crush the pride of ancient lore.

Oh! Castlereagh, false Castlereagh!
Fed offspring of the tyrant's sway,
A mother's rights you did deny—
You snatch'd from her the cup of joy,
And in her hour of peace and pride
You plung'd the dagger in her side.

With icy lips and languid voice,
Whilst yielding to ambition's choice,
No country, or no God had'st thou,
When Saxon laws you did avow;
Yet such ambition could not save
Thy body from a bondsman's grave.

LINES DEDICATED TO THE MEMORY OF JOHN O'MAHONEY.

An honor'd chieftain's soul has fled—
A gallant son of fame
Who nurs'd the love of Erin's hopes
And gloried in her name;—
Whose heart intoned the echoing notes of free-
    dom's joyful tone,
Which swept the chords of Tara's Harp, when
    England was unknown.

Another brilliant mind of love
Is dimm'd by death's decree,
And hallow'd thoughts like visions bright,
Unborn though they be,
No more can wrap his fancies in the beauties of
    each tone,
Which noted angels' messages of freedom for
    his own.

Another flower of freedom's growth
Is cull'd from Erin's green;

7

And all its fragrant loveliness
Which beautified the scene,
No more can cast its petal bloom on time's
    momentous shore,
But yet, its grand magnetic power shall live in
    golden lore.

Another shamrock from the soil
Of Ireland's ancient race,
Through the destroying hand of death
No longer takes his place—
The children of his own dear land, wherever
    they may be,
Shall drop a tear in silence for their loved
    O'Mahoney.

THE SIEGE OF DUNBOY.

For fifteen days the English troops,
Over five thousand strong,
Beneath the walls of Old Dunboy,
The siege had to prolong;
That famous chief McGeoghegan,
Whose name shall never die,
With seven times twenty Irishmen
Was all that held Dunboy.

But fearless as the men of yore,
Which Sparta once had seen,
Was this brave band of patriots
Of Erin's native green:
Determin'd to resist such force,
They went to work with joy,
Unmindful of the dangers which
Appear'd around Dunboy.

A battery of five cannon
Before the walls was raised;
Incessantly their thunders roar'd,
Unceasingly they blaz'd.

Part of the castle tumbled down,
The English ran to try
To force an entrance, but they fell,
That day before Dunboy.

The batt'ry still kept up the fire
'Till the old vault fell in,
Enveloping beneath its ruins
Some gallant, faithful men;
The Britons then in crowds began
The breach to man on high,
But Irish soldiers cut them down
Once more, before Dunboy.

A third attack no better proved
Than the two made before,
Although they gained the castle hall,
They fled its walls once more.
" Undaunted sons of Irish sires,"
What hosts you did defy—
Did ever mortals fight before
Like those within Dunboy.

The President of Munster see'ng
The bold defence they made,

A fourth onset, far better planned,
He ordered with fresh aid;
The cannon still kept belching forth
Red iron-hail t' annoy,
Those warriors brave defending
The castle of Dunboy.

When the walls of the castle fell,
The English force began
With numbers overwhelming,
The recent breach to man;
The Irish stood like sturdy oaks,
Their weapons still to ply
In defence of their honor and,
The castle of Dunboy.

But they were forced to yield at length
To o'erpowering troops,
Who rushed upon the breach as thick
As grasshoppers in groups;
Yet with a desperation they,
The red-coats did defy,
Until the " Johnny Bulls " once more
Were forced out of Dunboy.

Although the brave *McGeoghegan,
Being wounded mortally,
Yet like another Achilles,
He still fought th' enemy;
Unmindful of his painful wound,
As Hector loved his Troy,
So fell this mighty chieftain brave,
At the siege of Dunboy.

The little garrison at length
Was overpower'd with men,
Who knew as little mercy as
The lion in his den;
But when our Irish soldiers brave,
For freedom 'gain shall try,
They'll teach those English blood-hounds what
They did within Dunboy.

---

* Richard McGeoghegan, who distinguished himself at the siege of Dunboy, although being mortally wounded the day previous to the sacking of the castle, still refused to listen to the terms proposed by the English for the surrendering of the garrison, as he well knew that no confidence could be placed on a government which had so often before disregarded its plighted word. When he saw the English rushing in crowded forces towards the entrance, he rose up although the grasp of death was tightening fast around him, and attempted to fire a barrel of powder that was near him, in order to destroy himself and the enemy, sooner than surrender to them. But he was prevented by Captain Power, in whose arms he was stabbed to death by the British butchering soldiers.

THE LIGHT OF ENGLAND'S GLORY 'S FLED.

The light of *England's glory 's fled—
The glory of her pow'r;
A faded streak of milky thread
Is all the former dow'r
That's left of greatness once proclaim'd,
A greatness oft dishonor'd, shamed
By vile, atrocious, blushing deeds;
Dark plots designed, when nature bleeds
From base intents—to crush the weak with
    hellish spleen,
Is all the greatness she has seen.

The fame of Britain, nursed so long
By vauntings ide, vain,
No more shall swell the nation's song
With ribaldries again;
The double-headed Eagle's swoop
Laid Turkey fainting in its coop;

* These lines were written when English diplomacy in regard to
the Eastern question was looked upon by other powers as very hu-
miliating.

The Lion gazed in sullen dread
Until the Eagle was well fed;
Then, crouching low, yet growling still, laid
 down
That title, to first-class renown.

'Tis well the force of truth at last
Breaks forth throughout the world,
The moon-shine of false fame is past,
And England's pow'r is hurl'd
From wild delusion's summit high,
To where the dregs of glory lie:
Despised for cowardly acts, too mean—
Dishonored in her own domain,
Looked down upon by nations small and great
To share, e'er long, the *" sick man's " fate.

---

* Turkey was called the " sick man " of Europe.

LINES DEDICATED TO THE HIBERNIAN RIFLES OF CHICAGO A. O. H.

Hail martial sons of sires of fame,
Immortalized the regiment's name
Shall stand, like the bright stars
From nature's lofty heights above,
Called down to shed light's golden love
Around the stripes which art express'd
With rainbow-smiles of gold impressed
Along the Banner Union gave,
To wave above the free and brave.

Hail sons of Jove's great war-like son,
Enthron'd in fame through glories won,
Make his great deeds your own;
Expressing wonder and surprise,
Let every nation's gaping eyes
Behold the force of pow'r each man
Throughout the gallant "Rifles" can
Surpass all others when called out
To share a nation's hope or doubt.

When angry clouds of war bedim
The brilliancy of freedom's gem,
Go shield its light divine,
Infuse the dark surrounding gloom
Which borrows shades from manhood's bloom
With the electric fire of fame,
Emitted from a soldier's name,
And whilst thy nation's love is known,
Her glories shall be yours alone.

THE IRISH PATRIOT'S ADDRESS.

Irishmen, sons of Irish sires,
Unforgotten in your martial deeds
Of undying fame and valor—
Why stand you thus idly abased?
And, as if it were thoughtlessly
Wallowing in the mire of slavery,
Subjecting your illustr'ous names
To the silent graves of bondsmen.
Alas! my own belov'd country—
Ah! false suggested idea,
Why should'st thou my muse inspire me
To proclaim, " Alas! my country!"
Because of her foes?   No, surely
I did but mouth; the dark, frowning,
Angry clouds, of murky hue,
Which dim'd the zenith of our fame,
Are dissipating fast away,
Receding towards the horizon,
Where the British Lion crouches

In sullen despair, as Irish
Soldiers make havoc in his lair.
Ah! perfidious pow'r of England,
Thy vile offspring (usurpation)
Never ponder'd for a moment
On the inflexible will of
Irish greatness, wherein now lies
The impending doom of Britain's
Humiliation, yielding to
The mighty conquering prowess
Of the proud children of the Gael.
Oh! England, vile, false, freebooting,
Marauding, vain and despotic
England, had'st thou but paus'd e'er first
Thy scampering feet polluted
The bloom of the tri-leaf'd shamrock,
And scann'd the stalwart forms of chiefs,
Whom Erin honored as her sons,
Thy march, inglorious onward,
Would have been impeded,
And the pregnant storms of lurking
Treachery, would never bedim
The sweet sunshine smiles of Ireland.
But the brilliant, sea-girt gem of

The mighty rolling Atlantic
Fired thy jealous heart, and kindled
In thy soul's imagination
A lustre, whose brilliancy could
Not reflect the diamond, without
The Em'rald gem of the surging
Billows of the expansive deep
To reflect its beauties on thine.
Inborn desire of uncouth reflection;
Thy heart's panting phantom
Nurs'd wild, fanciful delusions,
Which seem'd to enthrone the name
Of England in historic lore,
As the famed conqueror of the
Great unconquer'd Irish Nation.
Surely 'twas but a delusion,
For old Ireland, though still bleeding
And crushed down with bull-dog fury,
Yields not to the base usurper,
Though the poison'd fangs of England's
Malice, with snake-like instincts, are
Ever ready to bury their
Deep-rooted evils in her heart.
Yes, my oppress'd and injured land,

Though still unconquered nation,
Thy faithless usurper scoffs at
Thy woes, and taunts thee in distress.
But thy children cannot forget
The frowning sneer of the scoffer;
The evils of centuries, serve
But to enkindle in their souls
A holy flame of undying fame,
Which their names shall ever bear to
Posterity, encaging the
Terrors of the ruthless tyrant
In the shades of oblivion.
The day of freedom is at hand,
That long wished for impassion'd day,
Which has smiled through the distress of
Ireland for seven hundred years;
Which alone kept the patriots'
Patriotism burning with love
Of fame, as it was to usher in
The sun of freedom, which had long
Before cast its bright, cheerful smiles
Of golden beauty throughout the land,
And sweetly bless'd a saintly race
Nursed in science and golden lore.

Yes, Irishmen, the day's at hand,
And England's downfall is marked on
The face of the orient sun.
As he transcendently ascends
The blue vault of heaven, to the
Dazzling zenith of his glory.
Let not the glory of that sun
Depart beneath the west'rn sky,
'Till the treaty-breaking tyrant
Shall crouch submissively at thy feet,
Supplicating mercy! mercy!
That mercy which she never knew.

THE MASSACRE OF WEXFORD.

Cromwell,* deluded by kingly assumption,
In deeds of horror enthroned his presumption—
The red-handed murders which stained his
    career
In darkness and death, 'round his grave shall
    appear.

His butchers alike for destruction were rife,
Like demons preparing to quench human life,
They mercilessly slaughter'd the young and the
    fair
With increasing joy, as they view'd their despair.

Their foul deeds polluted the green mantling
    soil
Which beautifies Erin with nature's soft smile;
But never had mortals so beastly as yet
Dishonor'd mankind as this inhuman set.

* Lingard says, in his description of the Massacre of Wexford, no
distinction was made by Cromwell between the defenceless inhabitants and the armed soldiers; nor could the shrieks of 300 females who
had gathered around the cross prevent them from the swords of those
ruthless barbarians.

When the armless, harmless men of the town
Were shot without mercy, those blood-hounds
    came down
With demon-like horrors express'd in their
    eyes,
To the great cross, from which 'rose the
    maidens' cries.

Those innocent fair ones, defenceless, alone,
Would melt hearts with pity, were they not of
    stone;
Oh! blush, human nature! Ah, God is it so?
They heed not those tears flow'ng from souls
    rent with woe.

Base monsters of hell's belching horrors of
    dread,
What demons your foul hearts with their vomits
    fed,
Which shamefully led you, wild beasts to ex-
    ceed
In bloody connection with this dreadful deed.

Oh! God, what a moment! what death-dealing
    strife,

8

Those females, like angels, are pleading for life,
Whilst the Saxons' steel with their hot blood is
    red—
The vengeance of tyrants with innocence fed.

Vile, baseless assassins, your dark deeds of
    blood,
Which crimsoned with horrors a nation so good,
Can never be wash'd from the pages of shame,
Like grim spectres 'round Britain's name they'll
    remain.

And when Irish valor again shall be tried,
Ah! surely the thoughts of those lov'd ones
    who've died
For the freedom of Erin, shall add to its might,
Until British glory is paled in its light.

A DIALOGUE BETWEEN CROMWELL AND THE BRITISH PARLIAMENT ON THE SACK OF DROGHEDA.

Crom.—"To your Honorable Body I bring tidings of another wreath of laureled victory, which shall add to the fame of our country."

Par.—"Another victory, did you say, O, Cromwell? Truly, that is gratifying to hear."

Crom.—"And in a more especial manner shall your Honorable Body rejoice, when I shall make known to you the sweeping current of unceremonious cruelties, which was my pleasant duty, to inflict on the inhabitants and soldiers of Drogheda."

Par.—"O, chivalrous chief, thy country shall bestow on thee encomiums which shall eclipse the brilliancy surrounding the name of the victorious Cæsar."

Crom.—"I thank your Honorable Body for those kind expressions, expressions which I shall always cherish as the unclouded sun of my existence."

Par.—" And dost thou not deserve the thanks
of a grateful nation for butchering those rebel-
lious Irishmen, whose very souls recoil with
abhorrence at the freedom of our generous
laws."

Crom.—"That is the very reason that the
angry whirlwind of my wrath became pregnant
with lurking treacheries. I held out promises
of pardon to all who should submit and lay
down their arms. But no sooner had I found
myself in peaceful possession of the garrison,
when I commanded my men to bury their bur-
nished bayonets and flashing sabres of steel
within the breasts of those doomed papists, to
whom, but a few moments before, I gave every
assurance of protection. But was it not better
and more honorable to break my word on such
an occasion, than to allow such mortals debase
humanity by their Popish ideas?"

Par.—" You are right, Cromwell. You have
the sanction of our laws, and you know our
laws are generous."

Crom.—" Relying on the confidence of such
laws, I felt it my duty to enforce the resolutions

passed by your Honorable Body on the 24th of October, A. D. 1644, when it was stated in unmistakable letters, that ' No quarter should be given to any Irishman, or to any papist born in Ireland.' "

Par.—" O, Cromwell! If Charles the First only observed our laws half as well as you do, we should not be compelled to steep the throne of England in the *gory tide of royalty.*"

Crom.—" The Parliament should be respected and its laws enforced, though the king's head should fall upon the scaffold. (To himself :) *' If I were king, I should execute the laws to suit myself, and then I should execute any minion who should dare to dictate to me. Oh! how I long for kingly robes and regal power.*' "

Par.—" Your words, O, Cromwell, are full of wisdom, and, without doubt, you have rightly served those unfortunate papists and rebels of Drogheda."

Crom.—" Let me explain to your Honorable Body how God blessed my endeavors at Drogheda. After battering, we stormed it. The enemy were about three thousand strong in town. I believe we put to the sword the whole number of the defendants. I don't think *thirty* out of the *whole number* escaped with their lives, and those who did are in safe custody for the Barbadoes. This has been a great, marvelous mercy. I wish that all honest hearts may give the glory of this to God alone, to whom, indeed, the honor belongs, for instruments, they were very inconsiderable to the work throughout."

"For five days after the surrender of the garrison, my men, through my orders, continued to butcher those defenceless prisoners, lest their Romish tenets should corrupt my brave soldiers. And in a more especial manner were my orders executed with zeal, when a number of ecclesiastics were discovered within the walls of the garrison. My soldiers, knowing how I despised and abhorred such persons, in consequence of their *religion* and *masterly abilities*, plunged their already gory-dripping weapons, to the hilt, into their bodies until the last flickering

NOTE.—Cromwell's Letters to Parliament.

rays of mortality were extinguished in agonizing groans. God nerved my hand to spill the *blood of papists.*"

Par.—" For this important victory, O, Cromwell, we shall appoint a day of thanksgiving to be held throughout the nation. You have merited our sincere thanks, and we entirely approve of the execution done by you on the *papists* of Drogheda, inasmuch as it is an act of justice to them, and mercy to others who may be warned by it."

Crom.—" It shall be my greatest pleasure during life to stamp out of existence everything Irish. They love their religion too much to become Puritans, and they are too brave to be allowed to increase. The only way England can hold her position in Ireland, is by crushing her inhabitants when they are not able to resist. Whilst they are prostrate is the time to strike. This is my policy, this is what I have practiced, and this is what I intend to carry out. The *magnanimous laws* of your Honorable Body give me every encouragement, and I shall

NOTE.—See Parliamentary History, Vol. III., p. 1,331.

always avail myself of the opportunity which
they offer in burying my sabre to the hilt in the
bodies of the Irish, regardless of *men*, *women*
or *children*. Alike they shall all fall beneath
my power. Our *generous laws* proclaim it
just, and *such justice* shall be meted to them."

Par.—"May God grant you to fulfill such a
mission. The Irish have always been a source
of trouble. They disclaim the idea of being
British subjects. No king or queen can conquer
them. Their patriotism is a dagger in the side
of the British Lion, and if you extract it, you
shall have done more for England than all
England herself can accomplish."

MOTHER ERIN SPEAKS:

Disturbers of my children's peace,
Your vile designs but swell
The contamination which surrounds
The crimes you love so well.
Take heed polluted Britishers;
The horrors which outline

Those evils which you've practiced long,
So oft, on me and mine,
Within the hearts of my loved sons
For ever shall remain,
Until they've paid you back in tons
Of tears, for your disdain.

The blasphemous expressions which
Knave Cromwell has express'd,
Would shame the great arch-fiend himself,
By whom he is possess'd.
The murders he has committed
Unpunish'd shall not go,
My valiant sons, remember well
That England is my foe.
The day of retribution yet
Shall dawn with crimsoned rays,
And England never shall forget
The mem'ry of those days.

And thou perfid'ous Parliament,
With all thy gen'rous laws,
Which sanction crime, without reserve,
To crush out freedom's cause.
The sword of justice shall dethrone

Each vicious, mad decree
Which you have always issued 'gainst
My children brave and me.
The glory of all former fame
From thee shall pass away,
And bless my ancient race and name
With light of freedom's day.

THE BLOODY CROWN OF ENGLAND.

The bloody crown of England no more shall
    rule our land.
The Saxon's footsteps shall be seen receding
    from our strand;
Like Cæsar on the battle-field, dispatching back
    to Rome.
Ireland shall yet proclaim the freedom of her
    home.

What trembling serf shall underrate the glory
    of our cause,

When liberty proclaims the right to crush out
    slavish laws?
The coward shall bow his head in shame and
    sink in slavery,
But Irishmen fear not to die, to leave Old Ire-
    land free.

Don your martial robes, my sons, and hasten to
    proclaim
The resurrected valor of old Erin's restored
    fame;
Let nations wonder at your power, as they have
    done of yore,
When, terror stricken and dismayed, the North-
    men fled your shore.

Bright shall the sun of vict'ry shine upon the
    Em'rald Isle,
When bloated Johnny shall forsake the glory
    of his spoil;
That land of golden lore which cast its beauties
    o'er his brow,
No more shall light the tyrant's face, it shines
    on freedom now.

EMMETT.

Why breathe not his name, 'tis the beacon of
    glory,
Which his patriotism to tyranny gave;
From father to son, 'tis transmitted in story,
It looms through the darkness 'round the pa-
    triot's grave.

In the pride of his youth like a beautiful flow'r,
Which bloom'd but to perish by the despoiler's
    hand,
Thus Erin, thy Emmet was crushed in his pow'r,
In defending the rights of his dear native land.

In his lone cell at night, each throbbing
    emotion
Which swept the loved strings of the old notes
    of time,
Evok'd in his heart a sad, holy devotion,
For his country's harp-notings, so grand and
    sublime.

The blood-stained usurper, dear Emmet, who
    bound thee,
And prejudg'd thee to death with a frown of
    disdain,
Could never dethrone the affections around
    thee,
Which thy country—though bleeding—shall
    always maintain.

Shall that nation which lov'd him, still languish
    and mourn,
When his spirit cries out with the patriot dead,
To strike for the freedom which England has
    torn
From the bosom of Erin, for which martyrs
    bled?

SAD! SAD WAS THE DAY.

Sad! sad was the day, when the freedom of Erin
Was dimmed in its glory by freebooting power,
When red-handed bigots demanded a share in
That land, where usurpers ne'er reigned for an
 hour;
When the men of the North were swept to
 destruction,
As if Hecla belch'd on them its dire eruption,
Engulfing forever each future pretension
To conquer the warriors of Erin-go-bragh.

Thy fame was unbroken, thy sons were united,
And thy heroes unmatch'd in the prowess of
 war—
Unbought by corruption, with virtue delighted,
The bright hopes of Erin shone forth like a
 star;
In the strength of their youth they fought with
 emotion,
To render their country the pride of the ocean,
Whilst bards indigen'ous sung songs of devotion
To Erin, loved Erin, Old Erin-go-bragh.

But, alas! belov'd country, disunion and strife
Overshadow'd thy beauties with mis'ry and woe,
And put into the hand of the stranger, the knife
To strike thy dear heart, a cruel, treacherous
    blow;
Oh! traitor McMurrough, thy country shall
    mourn
As long as her harp remains sad and forlorn,
And her shamrock, by Britons be tramped with
    scorn—
For thy hand sow'd disunion in Erin-go-bragh.

Yet the tyrant who binds thee, my country, no
    more
Can keep thee in bondage, if thy children arise
And recall to their memories the deeds of yore,
Which their sires in the time of their greatness
    did prize.
Belov'd land of my fathers, unconquer'd as yet,
The cruel, lawless stranger who crush'd thee
    may fret,
For the blood he has shed we shall never for-
    get:
'Till England is vanquish'd by Old Erin-go-
    bragh.

WHAT ARE IRELAND'S PROSPECTS NOW?

What are Ireland's prospects now, from land-
　　lordism dread?
Shall tyrants still avow the miseries they've
　　bred,
Like foul pollution, spreading its blasting views
　　alone,
When virtue's shining brilliancies appear
　　fore'er gone?

'Tis hard to understand what issues are in
　　store
For those who till the land, in Erin's sad green
　　shore;
Rulers there dishonor worth, and shield free-
　　booters when
Other nations on this earth call them dishonest
　　men.

What can a nation do when thieves upon her
　　prey,

And tyrants still renew the despot's former
    sway;
When the minions of the law become a lawless
    band,
And justice hides dishonor'd beneath corrup-
    tion's hand?

'Tis hard, indeed, to tell, the pregnant future's
    child
May bless C. S. Parnell with prospects grand
    and mild,
Or storm nature at its birth with gaping jaws
    of ire,
Emitting from destruction's breast blasts of
    burning fire.

The force of pow'r alone uniting hearts and
    hands,
Can monarchs vile dethrone, and all their base
    commands
Shall vanish like the blasts of hyperborean
    wrath,
Remembered but for the ills, destructions, which
    they brought.

9

The gloom which shrouds the hour of morning's
    freedom sun,
Shall melt before the pow'r of deeds of glories
    won,
And cradle happiness and fame in smiles of
    beaming love,
Surrounded with those blessings, bestowed by
    God above.

That hour is near at hand, prepare, brave, gal-
    lant men,
To wed your native land, and be her pride again
With hearts and souls proclaim, through
    union's strength, your cause,
And every nation's fame shall ring for you
    applause.

The peaceful smiles of bliss shall light your
    glories on,
And sun-shine beauties kiss the graves of heroes
    gone;
These are thy prospects Erin now, dear mother-
    land of mine,
May God enthrone thy glories with His great
    hand divine.

LINES WRITTEN ON THE OCCASION OF THE INCARCERATION OF THE HON. CHARLES STEWART PARNELL.

Exalted chief, in thy chains we admire thee,
And feel every pang in thy cell which is thine,
We think of the dread, lurking horrors 'round
thee,
Which tyrants hoard up to crush each free
design.

The sweet, lovely germs which feed thy affec-
tion,
To regenerate thy loved nation with love,
Could not take root in the wiles of subjection—
It springs from the essence of freedom above.

Enthroned in thy heart's deep 'motions, loved
Erin,
Surrounded with chains, lay reclining in tears;
Son-like responding, such sorrows to share in,
Or unbind the chains which have bound her for
years.

The blood-stained usurpers who've murder'd
  our sires,
And laughed at their miseries with scornful jest,
Grow pale with anxiety, lest thy desires
Should nurse love of hope in each Irishman's
  breast.

Like thieves in the night they broke thy calm
  slumbers,
And bound thee in irons for love ever thine—
They dread'd its effects on patriot numbers
Might rouse them to glory for freedom divine.

MY NATIVE LAND.

Sweet lovely island, fairest of nature,
Though fragrance breathes through thy dewey
    flow'rs,
Thy hills are clothed with usurpation
Which mars the peace of thy tranquil bow'rs;
The tyrants sway there knows not perfection,
But begets sorrows which often swell
Within the hearts of the sons of Erin,
Whilst tears respond to each sad farewell.

Those verdant valleys where feather'd warblers.
With silvery notings fill'd the pure air,
No more can cheer the son of the muses,
Who oft was wrapt in bright scen'ries there;
Home of my childhood, thy thoughts are dearer
Within my heart than my muse can tell,
'Tis through my love, I was forced to leave
    thee,
And say with sorrow, dear land, farewell!

Oh! rare clad mountains, hills of St. Patrick,
Your summits sip the celest'al dews,
As if to show an approximation
To wide expanse of ether'al views;
Dear native island, thy fame and glory,
Like sister stars yet, light up each dell,
Though British tyrants have tried to shadow
Their brilliant rays with the smoke of hell.

Triumphant greetings which oft extol'd thee,
Now lie submerg'd in thy children's tears,
But the usurper who mocks their weeping,
Rests not the night from surrounding fears;
Yes, well might Britain look 'round and
    tremble.
The stings she gave are remember'd well,
The sons of Erin are not forgetful—
Revenge seeks vengeance where tyrants dwell.

THE MAIDS OF ERIN.

Sweet lovely maidens of Erin,
Your blushes of purity glow
Like the pure lamp-light of virtue,
Far fairer than blood upon snow.

What beauty can equal the charms
Of Erin's lov'd daughters so mild,
Innocence, truth and devotion,
They cling to, as much as the child.

What virtue and sweet affection
Dwell in their rolling blue eyes,
Their voice-like soft notes of music,
Sounds magic-like even in sighs.

Calm lovely daughters of Erin,
Your virtue is grafted in fame,
Some maidens your charms might equal,
But none, your devotion can claim.

THE HOME OF MY YOUTH.

In disconsolation, I wander forlorn
From the friends of my youth who once
    cherish'd me kind,
And the home of my childhood where oft I
    planted
Sweet jasmine roses with a light buoyant mind.
Now, no longer I gaze with fond admiration
On that lovely green cottage, my day dream of
    yore—
Its beauties my memory shall ever awaken,
Though the wide foaming ocean between us
    shall roar.

How fleet were the moments to me as I linger'd,
When the last rays of Phœbus adorned the
    West.
What youthful emotions of joy I experienc'd
In the bosom of friends, I loved dearest and
    best.

Each evening at twilight whilst soft winds were
    blowing,
And the landscape before me was charming to
    view,
I sat by the side of my dear loving mother
'Till the sweet flow'rs of summer were laden
    with dew.

How sweet were the hours whilst her soft
    beaming glances,
Like the bright smiles of Luna, looked kindly
    on me—
Her gentle caresses I fondly remember,
When bowing at the alter of death's sad decree.
How lonely I watched her when life was de-
    parting,
Every pulse of my heart beat heavy with woe,
Whilst sadly her cold lips I pressed with
    devotion,
As the tears from my eyes like a fountain did
    flow.

IRELAND.

Sweet land of my fathers, for ages, through
    ages,
Fair Eden with charms of sweetness thine own,
Where now are thy heroes, thy statesmen and
    sages?
Have they left thee in bondage to struggle
    alone?

The glory which fame shed its lustre around
    thee,
Like transcendent greetings of heavenly bliss,
No longer illumes all those virtues around thee,
Which chivalry sealed with an immortal kiss.

The polluted touch of the freebooting stranger,
Has blighted those sun-smiling glories of fame,
The dark brooding evils of tyrants endanger
The life of those loved ones, who cling to thy
    name.

But England shall feel that the glory of Erin,
Though shrouded by tyranny's spectres of
     dread,
Shall rise through the pow'r of her own be-
     loved, wherein
The spirit of fame throughout ages was bred.

Lov'd Erin, thy sons are as brave yet as ever,
Their every heart's pulse is a life sign for thee,
They wait but the moment thy cruel chains to
     sever,
And lead thee triumphant to sweet liberty.

POUGHLUE EYON.

INTRODUCTION TO POUGHLUE EYON.

Tradition has carefully nursed the wild, romantic stories which breathe the mysteries of Poughlue Eyon.

Long before the missionary labors of St. Patrick, it was customary for the Irish people to offer their tributes of praise, thanksgiving and adorations to idols. The sun, as the grandest of all visible objects, was acknowledged their Supreme Being. History records the fact of the Irish Druids lighting fires, and driving their cattle between them, that they might escape any contagion which should arise in the island. These fires they called Belltaine and Baltine, that is, the fire of the god of Baal.

At the time, when the facts narrated in the following poem occurred, the people were extremely superstitious, and to such an extent did they inculcate its principles in the minds of their children, that, even in the present day in

Ireland, among the more ignorant of the peasants, a spirit of this former superstition stalks abroad in unmistakable evidence of its traditional nature.

About nine miles east of the city of Limerick (the city of the broken treaty) a beautiful mound, from an unbroken plane, rises itself aloft until its summit, five hundred feet above the level of the sea, looks proudly down on one of the grandest landscapes of nature, known to the inhabitants of the county, as the "golden vale." This beautiful country, like a vast extended fairy-lawn, ravishes the eye with its purest emerald, while the daisies bespangle its bosom with their lovely hues of red and white, adding an expressive grandeur to the scene. On the other side, a marshy waste spreads itself out in a northerly direction, and casts a rather sombre, shadowy gloom around the base of the mound, as if some lurking, unawed hobgoblings dwelt in the bosom of its treacherous aspect.

A tributary of the Shannon waters its base with its silvery ripplings, and sanctifies the scene, with the almost silent murmurings of its peaceful waters. On the top of this hill, beneath the foliaged boughs of the Irish oaks, a dark, dread cavern sinks its shaft of unfathomed space through the bowels of his moundship, as if a bolt from Jove's right arm, hurled with the vengeance of an angry god, tore from its crested pride, some imagined foe hid beneath the recesses of its interior depths. So appears the yawning abyss which opens with sepulchre-like shape on the very summit of this hill, traditionally known as " Poughlue Eyon."

An old Irish clan of the name of Eyon, for centuries occupied that part of the country. They worshipped the sun as the great god who swayed the universe, and directed everything according to the dictates of his almighty power. He it was, they believed, who, in the transcendent glory of his animated nature, caused this cave to shaft the mound, to light up a subterranean rivulet, which flowed from its base in mystic meanderings into the queenly Shannon, as it proudly swept the boundary of Limerick in its course to the mighty Atlantic.

This princely race of Milesian extraction, held

undisputed sway over half of Limerick for
hundreds of years, until a wild, half savage
tribe from Normandy, brought hither in quest
of plunder, in one dread night, while sleep
calmed in its peaceful sweetness the entire
community, they fell victims of an unholy conquest to the barbarian hosts who swept over
their country, and left but two to tell the tale
of that bloody carnage, which obliterated the
power and glory of the proud chiefs of the
clan of Eyon. One was the oldest son of the
reigning chief, Adrastus Eyon, who was
married the previous night to Irena McMore,
the daughter of a Munster chief, whose beauty
and virgin modesty veiled her lovely form, like
the crystal dew drops bathing the fairest lily
with glistening purity.

They had just retired from the banquet-hall
of his father's castle, to his own princely court,
when his valet, in breathless anxiety, rushed
into his bed chamber, and hastily told him of
the massacre of the chiefs of his race; then,
with all the alacrity of a faithful servant, he
rushed into the court-yard, and pushed his way

with a determined purpose to the hostelry, and prepared two horses for his master and lady. With these he returned to the mansion-house, where the chieftain and his bride, eagerly mounted their steeds and fled from their sumptuous halls in the darkness of the night, like condemned criminals.

Disguised as peasants, on the following day they sought a glen, which afforded them a safe hiding place from the ruthless stranger. Here they were warned in a dream to reside, until an avenger from their race would smite the barbarous foeman. Guided by the inspiration of this dream, they settled down to abide the wishes of the gods. In the course of time a son was born to them, and he was called after his murdered grandfather, Adrastus Eyon. His mother, one of the most accomplished scholars of the age, instructed her youthful son in four or five different languages, amongst them, the Norman tongue, which she herself had learned from her mother's uncle, a nobleman of Frankish origin. Two other children were born to them, but they died very young, leaving Adrastus the sole heir of a usurped province.

10

These are the material facts from which the following poem derives its existence. They were furnished to the author by his esteemed and worthy friend, Michael W. Ryan, Esq., to whom, as a mark of respectful courtesy, it is dedicated, with the seal of friendship of

P. C. T. B.

POUGHLUE EYON.

A meadow'd mound on Eyon's plain
In classic grandeur deck'd the scene,
And rear'd its head with lofty mien
In proud defiance o'er the green.
In ages past tradition gave
A history to this shamrock'd hill,
How Druidic gods, there sunk a cave,
To light a subterran'an rill.
Olympic-like, extolled in name,
Its glories filled the nation's rhyme:
The bards immortal flashed its fame
Throughout the land, in every clime.
The golden vale in mantled green,
Like fairy lawns extending wide
From its peaked summit, grand, serene.
Was seen around on every side.
Its Em'rald steeps bespangl'd o'er
With daisies beautifying its hue,
Gave it romantic looks which wore
An aspect ever strange, and new.
Large spreading oaks enthron'd their poise
Around its lofty summit, and

Enhanc'd its beauty with their size,
Until the scene was truly grand.
'Twas here the Druidic priests of yore
Sang praises to the god of Baal,
Whilst sages, bards and warriors bore
Tradition's lore through camp and hall.
The measur'd steps of chiefs and men,
Were heard upon its summit high,
When Sol's bright orient rays set in
To golden the blue Eastern sky.
Deep through this mound a chasm ran,
With yawning dread, it opened wide—
A wild romantic gap which man
Had never dared within to hide.
Its dark dread gaping depths, unknown,
Were filled with fancied horrors wild,
Where mortals once were basely thrown,
Who dared to have their gods reviled.
Its craggy edges moss'd with time
Are shadowed over, whilst the breeze
Yet, palls its myst'ries, nursed in crime,*
By trembling shadows from the trees.

---

* Whenever any of the inhabitants profaned the god of Baal, they were thrown into this poughlue, or cave, as a punishment of their disbelief.

Within engulfing depths below,
A strange, blue mystic brook runs on,
Commission'd by the gods to flow
Into the deep, winding Shannon.
Once in a time, e'er Ireland woke
From paganism's slumbering spell,
A vision of love's sweetness broke
Through the lone solitude which fell
Around the lonely, lowly cot,
Where Eyon lived in days of yore,
Beloved by gods, by men forgot—
A stranger in his native shore.
His parents lived in guilded halls,
Where the broad Shannon's silvery tide
Wash'd the strong butments of their walls,
As it swept onward in its pride.
For centuries untold they sway'd
The country 'round, no other man
Could have such strength, or force display'd,
As could the chieftain of this clan.
But a rude, savage, wand'ring race,
Equipped, well-armed, fill'd the land,
Their dreadful deeds soon left no trace
Of this brave, gallant, pow'rful band.

When the drawn shades of sable night
Encurtained nature with its hue,
This fierce nomadic tribe's delight
Was wild, when Eyon's hosts they slew.
In one dread hour this bloody deed
Of horrors red with streaming gore,
Like vengeance blasted Eyon's seed—
Proud scions of the land no more.
A wild, dread, savage yell arose
Above the Em'rald, golden vale,
As from the recking of death's throes,
They left but two to tell the tale.
These were the chieftain's younger son
And his dear, newly-wedded wife;
A couple who had scarce begun
To realize a marriage life.
The glories of new joys arose
Before this happy, youthful pair,
When, through those blood-stained foreign foes,
They were shut out in dark despair.
Wanderers from their peaceful home,
Where bounty lavished golden store,
They knew not where they dared to roam,
Oppressed with wrongs, from comforts tore.

Yet mindful of the tender life
That was entrusted to his care,
Young Eyon battled brave through strife
Through cherished love for her, so fair.
Within a craggy glen, secured
By forest oaks, they built a cot;
To hardships never yet endured,
They settled down to bear their lot.
'Twas here the hero of this tale
First opened his bright infant eyes,
And learned of his parents wail
With deep emotions of surprise.
His father tilled a little lot
Of table-land beside the glen,
Determined that his home should not,
Though rude, be lost to comforts, when
His loving wife and child were there,
Dependent on his daily toil:
He sought his work with anxious care,
As if unmindful all the while
Of the rude shock which blighted all
The comforts of his youthful life,
He only felt that in his fall
He had to live for child and wife.

To boyhood's years the infant grew,
His mother stored his mind with lore
Until his master gen'us knew
The languages and sci'nce before
The sun of twenty summers lent
Its golden smiles to warm his brow,
Whilst yet his soul seemed ever bent
To sword the wrongs he suffered now.
One peaceful eve when Sol had waned
His golden features from the West,
E'er yet pale Luna's rays had beamed
With peaceful sweetness—lured from rest,
Young Eyon wander'd far beyond
The confines of his lowly home;
In dreamy thoughts his spirit scanned
New scenes he had not dared to roam.
His soul was filled with raptures wild
As childhood scenes his father knew,
Described to him when yet a child,
Before his fanci'd vision threw
Their seasoned beauties of the past
Around his troubled soul at last;
"Ah me!" he sighed, "this wooded lawn,
And yonder castle tow'ring high,

Were ours alone, until this spawn
Of savage Normans, crowding nigh,
Like a dread tempest swept the land,
When peaceful slumber closed the eyes
Of Eyon's proud unconquered band,
Until, thus taken by surprise.
You gods immortal, hear the pray'r
Of the lone remnant of that race,
Whose glories you were wont to share
When shouts of triumph rent this place;
Nerve me with pow'r to meet the foe,
In god-like action in this field
Where my ancestors blood did flow,
That I may make the tyrant yield."
Thus had he pray'd on bended knees,
When on the gentle zephyr's tide
An angel's voice from yonder trees,
Came borne with unconscious pride.
Its rich soft cadence filled the plain
With harmony, to him unknown,
The gods themselves could not refrain
From ecstasies wrought by its tone.
His earnest, pray'rful voice was stilled,
The vengeance which had primed his soul,

No more its deep recesses filled—
That voice seemed destined to control.
It lured him on with eager pace.
Until he reached the fairy bow'r
Where sat that nymph of Norman race—
The daughter of that prince whose pow'r
Arose when Eyon's hosts were slain,
And left upon the tented plain.
Within a latticed bow'r she lay
Reclining on a rustic seat,
A youth beside her full of play.
With clapping hands her songs would greet.
"One other one, dear Ianno,"
Young Rudolph to his sister said,
"And I will keep as still, you know,
As mamma says, when I'm in bed."
"This is the last then, Rudolph, say
You will not ask me to sing more,
The Irish ghosts may come this way—
Papa said he saw 'em before."
Scarce had she spoken when, behold!
A shadow swept across the door,
Her voice was still'd, her blood ran cold,
As she stood trembling on the floor.

Young Eyon saw the shock he gave
That lovely, tender maiden fair,
Then anxiously inclined to save
That innocent young happy pair,
He stepped within the latticed bow'r
And spoke in softest, kindest tone:
"Sweet lovely maiden do not cow'r,
I am like you—of flesh and bone—
I would not hurt one golden hair
Of those rare, precious locks so fine;
No mortal could one moment dare
Dishonor one pure look of thine.
Enchanted by your voice, I came
Across yon lovely spreading lawn,
Resistance for me had no claim,
You would the gods themselves have drawn.
How could I then forbear to see
That lady of exquisite tone?
I pray forgiveness now of thee,
And I'll retire from here, unknown."
He ceased to speak, his hazel eyes
With looks of deep affection bent,
Awoke her from her strange surprise,
Whilst to her cheeks, the rose-hue went.

The sun of eighteen summers still,
With smiling sweetness warm'd her brow,
And hallow'd her blue eyes until
Their lustre shone with rad'ance now.
Her eyes a moment met his own,
That look was all, and yet it told
Of sentiments of bliss, unknown
To mortals wed to stores of gold.
With blushes deep she tried to say:
"Young man, I freely do forgive
The motives which led you this way—
Go sir! begone! if you would live,
My uncle comes this way. Oh! sir,
He will not have excuses when
He sees you here, he will infer
That you're a spy from Irishmen;
He is no lover of your race,
He would imprison and destroy
Each Irishman found in this place,
I pray good sir, hear me, fly! fly!"
Her anxious look, her tender care
Of him, so filled the young man's heart,
That he determined none should dare
To make him play a cowardly part.

"Fair lady, let me here remain,
Your uncle is already nigh—
One cowardly act shall never stain
My soul; here let me live, or die."
Scarce had he ceased to speak when, lo!
A chieftain of the Norman race
With stern voice said: "Ianno,
How came this stranger to this place?
Has he offended thee? if so—
The sharpness of this sword shall feel
His heart, and through its vitals go
Until his life blood stains its steel."
A dark frown settled in his look,
And lit his eyes with evil glance,
As if some demon's vengeance took
Possession of his fiery sconce.*
"My uncle, pray look not thus fierce,
This man has not insulted me;
No! no, your sword shall never pierce
This young man's heart, let him go free."
Thus spoke young Ianno the fair,
With supplicating hands between
Her uncle and the stranger there—

---
* Red hair.

Like some enchanted fairy queen.
" Whence is this visit then?" he said,
" What does his message here portend?
No stranger shall these precincts tread,
Unless he proves himself a friend."
Two guardsmen summoned, quickly came,
And stood before the open door,
The Norman chief then asked his name
With a contempt which malice bore.
His sneering frown and haughty tone
So filled young Eyon's soul with fire,
That he determined all alone
To brave this man of savage ire.
" Adrastus Eyon is my name,
My sires had lived and owned this place,
The world-wide had known their fame,
And I am of that honored race.
No dark dishonored deed befouls
Their graves dug by the strangers' hands.
When fury swelled the savage howls
Which rose above their murdered bands.
Alone I stand here—three to one,
No shining lance or blade I wield,
But mortal man had never won

That fame, which yet could make me yield.
This lovely tender maiden's song
Entranced my heart with joys unknown,
Unconsciously I came along,
Wrapt in the sweetness of her tone.
Within this fairy bow'r she sat
Reclining on that rustic seat,
My soul was so enamored that,
I had determined to retreat
Whilst Luna's orb was hid from view,
Behind yon fleecy murky cloud,
When, suddenly it rising threw
My shadow on the floor—a shroud-
Ed corpse exhumed from yonder grave.
Could never chill the heart's control
Of active pow'r, as thus I gave,
Unconscious to the lady's soul.
Could I retire and leave her there
A prey to fancied phantoms wild?
My soul would not such actions share
When I could quiet the maid and child.
I entered in, and briefly told
The lady of my visit here:
My mission was not pelf, or gold,

But this young maiden's song to hear.
For this alone, I am subject
To base insinuations now;
Shall I be thus a vile suspect,
And still, my manhood not avow?
Ah! though your guards had filled the plain,
I would assert myself as free;
The soul of cowardice I disdain,
'Twas never yet in mine or me."
" By the great gods your heart shall feel
The strength of arm I command;
A Norman's sword your life shall steal,
Thou minion of a worthless band.
Go Ichius,* give him thy sword,
In mortal combat to contend,
This insolence I can't afford,
He shall no longer here offend."
The guard obeys his master's word,
His short broad sword to him he gave,
Then ey'ng him, said: "you'll not have stir'd
From here, until you'll find your grave."
" Hold babbler, forgo thy prate,
Thy master's vauntings I defy,

* One of the guards.

No Norman, though however great,
Can force me from the field to fly."
Then turning towards the Norman chief,
With proud defiance in his eye,
He calmly said, " this will cause grief
To that young lady standing by.
Let us repair behind yon wall,
Where she cannot the combat see,
Yet, for her sake, you shall not fall,
Although I may a victim be."
Rudolphus grinned with scornful laugh,
As he addressing Eyon said·
"The gods their nectar shall not quaff
Until my sword shall cleave your head."
His haughty manner grieved the heart
Of the pale, tender Ianno,
Who begged the stranger might depart
Without be'ng thus molested so.
With flashing eyes Rudolphus cried:
" Your pleadings, madam, are in vain;
Here Ichius, take this maid aside,
Why does she in this place remain!"
" My father, sir," said Ianno,
" Shall hear this insult offered me;

11

To him, with this young man I'll go,
He shall despite your ire go free."
Ichius now advanced to take
Young Rudolph, and the maid away,
But Eyon, for the lady's sake,
Caused him beneath her feet to lay.
Oswald* then with drawn sword,
Subservient to his master's word,
Came forth, his honor to uphold;
But he, too, found that he had err'd—
With skill displaying a master's hand,
Adrastus with unerring stroke,
This other Norman had unmanned,
When at the hilt, his sword he broke.
Then, with one piercing look he said:
"Thy blood this cold steel shall not stain,
If you are not by tyrants lead,
This lady to insult again."
Rudolphus seeing the humble plight
Of his two guardsmen, thus did say
With irony: "young man you might
A thousand of my soldiers slay.
I'll not seek here, now, for redress,

---

* Another of the guards.

Nor shock my neice or nephew more,
But you shall answer yet for this
Before to-morrow's sun is o'er."
"Agreed sir; I am not the man
To harrow the young lady's soul,
Nor shall one mortal—whilst I can—
A single act of hers control.
I'll go with you to meet the chief—
The lady's father, though I die—
His words alone shall bring belief
Of what his thoughts of me imply."
Thus Eyon spoke in manly tone,
In princely aspect as he stood
In that green ivy house alone,
Contending against Norman blood.
Young Ianno with pallid face,
Yet trembling like a lily leaf,
Between the two still held her place
With Rudolph trying to soothe her grief.
Within his little hands her own
In softest pressure were caressed,
Whilst she would oftentimes stoop down
To press him to her tender breast.
At length her uncle led the way

In company with Adrastus and
The tender youth and maid, as they,
Walked close beside them, hand in hand.
The other two brought up the rear
With straggling footsteps, slow,
In deep unbroken silence near
Their chieftain and his daring foe.
" Here is our chief," Rudolphus said,
" To him I bring thee at thy word,
Or else my sword would soon have shed
Thy blood before thou would'st have stirred."
Reginald, the warrior Norman sat
On a large cushioned easy chair,
Within a mirrored saloon that
Seemed ablaze with chandeliers there.
He looked a man of savage mien,
A bushy beard, half brown and gray,
As strong as any horse's mane,
Stole nearly all his looks away.
A man of fifty years he seemed,
Of muscular appearance still,
And though his eyes with passion gleamed,
He showed an aspect of good will.
" If thou art chieftain of this place,"

Said Eyon calmly looking him,
" I am one of a fallen race,
Brought here through this man's idle whim.
Of what offence I am accused,
Let him who brought me here declare,
And it your laws I have abused,
Your judgments I shall calmly bear. "
Rudolphus then with angry voice,
Accused him as an Irish spy,
Who tried to play a shrewd devise,
And then when caught, now dares to lie.
He then accused him, how he tried,
With cunning words to play his part,
By counterfeiting manners—pride,
In trying to win his neice's heart.
Reginald grasped his dagger sword,
Whilst vengeance burned in his eye;
" Villain! " he said, " I can afford
To hear you yet before you die."
Fair Ianno, with trembling hands
Upraised before her father, said:
Oh, sire! beloved of these broad lands,
Let not this young man's blood be shed.
He has committed no offence

Against your daughter, or your laws,
See, father! see his innocence—
Against him there is not one cause."
Her hair in golden ringlets fell
Dishevelled on her snowy neck,
Her heaving bosom seemed to tell
The sorrow of some angel wreck.
"My daughter, why thus look so wild!
If this young man has ought to say
To prove his innocence, my child,
He shall go free from here away."
Her father pressed her to his heart,
Her angel sweetness moved him now,
Then with a love, which joys impart,
He kissed her pale, young anxious brow.
Young Eyon then imparted all
The circumstances through which he
Was led within this princely hall:
Being thus deprived of liberty.
Reginald heard the young man out,
Then turning to Rudolphus said,
"This man is innocent, no doubt,
He seems to me to be well-bred;
Conduct him to the castle hall,

Provide him bountiful to-night,
To-morrow Ianno shall call
And lead him forth to freedom's light."
Thus spoke the chief, young Ianno
With raptures kissed her father's lips,
Her heart with greater ease beats slow,
As from his love, her joys she sips.
Adrastus seemed to think his soul
Had wandered to some land of dreams
Where magic charms life control,
And love like golden sunshine gleams.
Like one arising from a trance,
Whose heart to virgin life awoke,
He to the maiden did advance,
As with expressive love he spoke:
"Fairest of mortal ladies, how
Can I express my thanks to thee!
Eternal love, my. soul I vow
Shall bless this cherished memory;
Not for my liberty I seek,
My humble thanks here to avow,
But for that soul, sublime, yet meek,
Which sanctifies thy lovely brow."
Then bowing before her father, he

Said: "Sir! this courtesy you've shown,
Shall never yet escape from me
Until its seeds have fruitful grown."
Thus say'ng, he gracefully retired,
Led by Rudolphus to the hall,
Where all the comforts he desired
Were his, with servants at his call.
These are thy quarters for the night,
The Norman said with mocking tone,
You can here, dream, to-morrow's light
Will find you in a land unknown.
Before young Eyon could reply,
Rudolphus pass'd beyond the door,
With vicious looks which might imply
A savage thirst for human gore.
Adrastus see'ng himself alone,
Soliloquizing thus, began:
" Where shall my parents think I've flown;
Or who can cheer them whilst I'm gone.
But yet to-morrow's sun shall shine
Around our cot within yon glen,
With golden love of light divine,
When I'm restored to them again."
Then rising to his feet he said:

" This Norman sword I got to-night,
I'll lay beside me on this bed,
It may be useful in a fight."
Then with a prayer for Ianno,
He to his peaceful couch withdrew,
Unconscious that his mortal foe
Through a crevice held him in view.
Rudolphus with a chuckle said:
" The hour of vengeance soon is mine,
Dream on thou mortal in that bed,
A cave of death shall soon be thine."
Then with a stealthy step he stole
To where his myrmidons had lain,
"Come on," he cried; " sleep holds control
Of him who would our race disdain.
He must be bound with seasoned cords,
His blood shall not besmear the hall,
Do not attempt to draw your swords,
Rush in and seize him—one and all."
Ten rustic, savage-looking men,
By him selected, cat-like crept
Around the couch, where peace had then
Smiled on young Eyon as he slept.
One moment they behold his face,

With eyes like demons glist'ning now—
A virgin smile had left its trace
Of sweetness stealing o'er his brow.
Ah! 'twas the smile which nursed his soul
In sun-shine of maternal joy;
A mother's love still held control
Of her dear, only, lonely boy.
But the rude savage fiend stood by,
A monster of sage insolence,
With malice burning in his eye,
What cared he for such innocence!
They seized and bound him like a thief,
Then with a conscious look of pride,
They turned to their ribald chief
Say'ng: "what shall to this man betide?"
With a chilled, cowardly laugh, he said:
"In yonder hill there is a cave,
Poughlue Eyon, let him there be led,
'Twill answer for a pleasant grave."
With shouts they led him up the hill
Until they gained the craggy steep,
Where Poughlue Eyon's shadows still
From dreary depths of chasms leap.
Into that gulf of horrors grim,

Which nought but dismal darkness knew,
To please their chieftain's savage whim,
This bloody band, young Eyon threw.

    *   *   *   *   *   *   *

The morning's sun found Ianno
As sweet as any flow'r could seem,
Smiling with love, anxious to go
Her Irish soldier to redeem.
She scarce could wait her morning meal,
So eager to depart was she;
She thought how lonely he would feel
Until he gained his liberty.
Then hurriedly, without escort
She found herself at castle hall,
But though she made an early start,
Eyon was gone, before her call.
With a sad, disappointed air,
She paced the hall where he had been,
Whilst yet another *lady fair
Approached her, wondering at her mien.
"My dearest cousin, Ianno
What seems to prey upon your mind,
Why! do you not Augusta know,
Or would you have me think you're blind.

---

* Augusta, the daughter of Rudolphus.

How is it that I find you here
Within this castle hall alone,
With countenance devoid of cheer,
As if your friends were dead and gone?"
"Excuse me, dearest cousin mine,
I came an noble soul to free—
A man for whom I would resign
My life to gain his liberty.
He is not here, I find him not,
What did your father with him do?
Tell me Augusta, have I got
A faithful sister still in you?"
" My dearest Ianno be calm,
You know Augusta's heart alone,
Would be my lovely cousin's balm
For ev'ry grief felt, and unknown.
I heard my father speak of one
Who seemed to be his guest last night;
Perhaps he'll tell you where he's gone,
See, here he comes, look not so white."
With courteous bow her uncle said:
"My lovely niece you have proved true,
But see, that wily fox has fled,
Unmindful of his vows to you.

His touching eloquence last night
Was playing a double traitor's part,
To win your love, he thought he might
Find freedom through your tender heart.
But now you see his base intent
For all the clemency you've shown,
Unconscious of your love, he went
Filled with presumption of his own."
"Thus let it be my uncle then,"
Said she, with a deep heaving sigh,
"I cannot judge his actions when,
Grave reasons might force him to fly."
Thus saying, Augusta's hand she took,
Whilst deep emotions still held sway
Within her bosom, yet her look
Seemed calmer as she went away.
Together to the fairy bow'r
Where she had seen him first they went,
"'Twas here," she said, " in a sad hour
My heart felt cold at his advent,
But with a sweet expressive tone,
He chased my childish fears away.
Oh! with such looks, as his, my own
Dear Augusta, what could I say?"

" Forgive him; yes, I did forgive—
He did not try to do me wrong,
Dishonor could not in him lie,
He only came to hear my song.
And yet your father seemed to rave
With some dread passion, uncontrolled,
As if he took him for a knave
Of complexed villainies untold."
She then related what took place,
With many child-like sighs of grief,
As if they could her heart embrace,
With tender hopes of love's relief.
" My dearest cousin Ianno,
Why should you fret yourself for him?
He is a stranger, you must know
That this is but the merest whim."
" Then let this whim be ever mine,
And though he be a stranger, yet
A vision of such love divine,
My memory never can forget."
In converse thus they sat for hours,
As if some magic sweetness there,
Held them entranced amidst the flow'rs,
Exhaling fragrance to the air.

*　　*　　*　　*　　*　　*　　*

A chill crept over Eyon when,
They threw him down that chasm dread,
As if his soul had left him then,
To wear a golden crown instead.
But when he felt the silent stream,
Which flow'd five hundred feet below,
He seemed to wander in a dream,
Through mystic scenes of death and woe.
He thought he saw the god of Baal
Surrounded by immortal bands,
As if they bore him in his fall,
Uplifted on their spirit hands.
With golden swords they cut away
The bands which bound him as he fell,
Whilst their looks, brighter than the day,
Shone 'round that grim sepulchered cell.
A life boat shaped with angel's wings,
Surrounded by a brilliant light,
Another ær'al spirit brings
Before his now bedazzled sight.
In this they oar'd him on the stream,
Which to the grand old Shannon led;
Where with a smile of crystal gleam,
The moon's rays softly lit its bed.

'Twas there the gods in solemn tone,
Commissioned Eyon in their name,
The tyrant stranger to dethrone,
And all his own lost rights to claim.
As if awakened from a trance,
Which mystified his very soul,
He seemed to grasp the magic lance,
Through which he should assume control.
With a determined purpose then,
He sought his humble cabin home,
His mother's sobs he heard within,
As if she thought he'd never come.
" You gods," she pray'd, " preserve my child,
The only offspring of his race—
Where have they from my love beguiled
My son, restore him to his place."
His father having searched in vain,
Returned to his lonely cot,
As if to ease his burning brain
From horrors which it seemed to plot,
But when he saw his son within,
Locked in his mother's fond embrace,
A peaceful smile of love again
Stole all the sorrow from his face.

Adrastus then imparted all
The events which caused his delay,
And how the gods, when in his fall,
Preserved his life, and cut away
The cords by which his limbs were bound,
As they consigned him to the cave,
Where those, despising the gods found,
At Druidic hands, a dreadful grave.
" Thus was your son preserved," he said,
" From the barbarian's vengeful ire,
As if arisen from the dead
Responsive to the gods desire;
I come to wield, in Erin's name,
The sword which hangs neglected now,
To tear from the rude stranger's fame
That pride which ill becomes his brow."
With marveled looks his parents then
Confessed to him their dreams divine,
Wherein one loved by gods and men
Would marshal warriors brave in line,
And lead them on in grand array,
Against that savage Norman band,
Until their power and bloody sway,
No longer cursed green Erin's land.

12

The morrow found Adrastus in
That grand old castle of McMore,
Which once defied the power of men
When Elim ruled the shamrock shore.
His grandfather received him well,
And fitted out a gallant corps,
With which he sought his native dell,
His lost possessions to restore.
His countrymen for miles around,
Who feared this Norman, savage band,
Marched to his standard as they found
A youth so brave who dared to stand
Against the bloody tyrant foe,
Who filled the land with every crime
Which breathed horrors wild and woe,
Foul offsprings of corruption's slime.
Then with this army on the plain
He pitched his tents, when sable night
Hid all the grandeur of this train
Within its dome of pale dim light;
But when the dawn of eastern sun
Awoke the Norman chief, to day
And saw what Irishmen had done,
He called his brother in dismay,

" What does this mean? Rudolphus, see,
The plain below is filled with men,
Go, call our soldiers instantly,
Those Irishmen shall bleed again."
Five thousand men in arms stood
Before their chieftain in an hour.
" My warriors brave of Norman blood,"
He cried, " We must assert our pow'r,
Again our swords shall cleave the way
To honor, victory and fame;
Before the sun sets on this day
Yon host shall bite the dust in shame.
One Irishman shall not escape
The vengeance of our polished steel,
This province with their dead we'll drape,
Their hearts our trusty blades shall feel."
Thus had he spoken, when there came
A horseman, plumed with green, in view,
Who thus addressed the chief by name,
" Reginald, I am sent to you,
Commissioned by our chief to say
That all your rights and titles here
Belonged to his old sept alway,
His undisputed claim is clear;

From hence you may retire in peace
If you resign to him his own,
But if resistance gives you lease
Of brighter hopes, lead your troops on."
Reginald, with a haughty sneer,
Made answer, " to your master fly;
Tell him the Normans know not fear
They live to conquer, not to die."
When Eyon heard the chief's reply
He called his gallant aids to him,
" The Normans," said he, " doth defy
Our pow'r, we now shall humble them;
Prepare, brave, valiant men, your clans,
To-day we march to victory,
The god of battle nerves our hands
Our country from her foes to free.
We might avenge our wrongs last night,
The same as they had done before,
But we will teach those tyrants right,
And thereby humble them the more.
When Eyon's god lights up the vale
And looks upon our gallant band,
That is the time for woe or weal,
To strike for our dear native land;

And now, that god looks brightly down
To bless our arms with his light,
Let his bright rays our glory crown:
Charge, onward, breast the foe in fight."
Three thousand men with one wild cheer
Responsive to that youth's command,
Rush'd to the contest without fear,
As they encounter'd, hand to hand,
The fiery Normans on the plain,
All eager for the bloody fray,
As tigers nursing hunger's pain,
Awaiting with fierce looks their prey.
Reginald led the vanguard host,
Although a man of senior years
His valor was the purchased boast
Of an unconquer'd tribe, whose cheers
Like pealing thunder shook the land
When his proud crest waved in the air,
Thus did this surging foreign band
Rush on his war-like deeds to share.
Rudolphus headed the right wing,
Although a moral coward was he,
Yet thinking what defeat would bring
He now charged with wild bravery.

Young Eyon on the other side,
Assisted by Donald McMore,
Like Jove's great sun in war-like pride,
Led on the gallant Irish corps.
In fierce contending ranks they met—
Their clashing arms rent the air,
Whilst death in dismal horrors set
His seal in mortals falling there.
Twice the Irish ranks were seen
To waver in that dreadful fight
'Till Eyon with his plume of green,
Like an avenging mars in sight,
Felled all who met him in the van,
Then rallying, at his power display'd,
This little army to a man
Shot death from every bloody-blade.
The Normans terror stricken fled,
Their chieftain sounded the retreat;
His brave invincibles lay dead
In thousands 'round his horse's feet.
Back to his castle still pursued,
The haughty chieftain and his men
Were driven, when, the fight renew'd
With more determined rage again.

Rudolphus with his column met
The advance of the enemy,
And though their ranks were broken, yet
They stood the charge with bravery.
Adrastus Eyon seeing his foe,
With fury in his youthful eye,
Made lanes of death with every blow,
Until he, to that chief drew nigh.
Then, thus addressing him, he said:
" Behold, thou bloody Norman fiend,
The young man whom you thought lay dead
In yonder cave, by you demeaned.
In contest let us here decide
To whom belongs the victory,
And may the rest in peace abide
When time 's no more, for you or me."
In dreadful conflict not before,
Had such contending heroes *met.
Their steeds, like Pegasus of yore,
Seemed winged with active movements, yet
Their riders fought with cautious care,
As if their very actions told
Those movements of their horses there,
Were feats of trained instinct of old

---

* Rudolphus, though a coward at heart, yet, on this occasion, displayed extraordinary courage, and was unquestionably a brave man when forced to fight.

Which warriors nursed with watchful zeal,
In colts designed for war alone
Until they were brought up to feel
The goaded spur to lead them on.
Rudolphus, with a warrior's skill,
Watched all the movements of his foe,
And met his every thrust, until
His helmet with one clashing blow
Fell severed from his head in two:
Then like a coward paled with fright
From the dread conflict there he flew
And saved himself by wretched flight.
Reginald seeing his brother fly,
And all his bloody clan dismay'd,
With vengeance lighting in his eye,
Broke, with a mighty oath, his blade—
" Thus let this contest end," he cried,
" The coward who would demean his race
Shall feel 'twas better he had died,
Than live and purchase his disgrace."
A few brave soldiers, faithful yet,
All, ready to obey his word,
Hung 'round their chieftain with regret,—
His heart touched by their love, was stirred:

"Soldiers," he said, " your vanquish'd chief
His grateful thanks to you extends
This pledge of love, more than his grief
Within his heart is felt, my friends.
Had all my men like you been true,
Our banner now should proudly wave—
But like a dastard horde they flew
And left us a dishonor'd grave."
" Not from the victor," Eyon said,
As he, approaching, heard the chief,
Then standing with uncover'd head,
He eased the old man's piquant grief,
" Thou bravest of the Norman race,"
Said he, " This victory of mine,
Which the great god of Baal did grace,
Shall not dishonor thee, or thine.
Although my royal father's lands
Were long, unjustly held by you,
Yet in this hour when peace commands,
I should not to myself be true
Could I forget, brave, generous chief,
Your daughter's kindness, and your own,
When you proffer'd me relief,
Although it was not after, shown."

The chieftain heard the young man's words,
Whilst the tears glistened in his eyes:
" This is," said he, " more than your swords
To me a far greater surprise;
Brave, generous youth, thou art indeed,
An honor to your country's fame—
And though a dark and bloody deed
Surrounds the lustre of my name,
Yet in the slaughter of your race,
No active part had I, or knew,
That such a massacre took place,
Until I gleaned the facts from *you.
In my own native land I held
A princely title and full sway,
'Till by a tyrant king expelled,
As I could not base laws obey.
My brother and my vassals all
Equipped, sailed over to your isle,
In conquest bent, or else to fall
And lie beneath your fertile soil.
To Albion, I fled at night,
My clans alone knew where I went

---

* When Eyon was taken before Reginald, on the night of his first
meeting with his daughter Ianno, it was then that Reginald was in-
formed from the lips of his prisoner of the massacre of his entire race.

'Twas there I heard with great delight
From the young man my brother sent,
That he had conquered Erin's pride,
The bravest chieftain in that land,
Whose soldiers all, fell by his side
A loyal, powerful, gallant band.
In language of expressive love,
He bid me hasten to your shore,
When peace and pow'r should always prove
My best companions evermore.
Thus had he pictured all to me,
And how he gained immortal fame—
When, a stranger to your country
Dismembered from my own I came."
Young Eyon's heart was filled with cheer
As he clasped the warrior's hand,
Saying, " Of that massacre you're clear,
And though a stranger in this land
Your every comfort shall be mine,
To guard with honor as a son,
Until that noble soul of thine
Shall gain immortal glories won.
Your tender son and daughter fair,
That lady whom I love alone—

Their princely father's home shall share
In yonder castle now your own."
In conversation thus they spoke
Until they reached the castle gate,
When a loud wail on their ears broke—
The inmates fear'd some dreadful fate
Would be their lot, as they beheld
The Irish soldiers marching through
Its portals, but their chieftain quelled
Their fears as he approach'd in view.
His daughter and his only son
Fell on his neck and wept aloud;
Their tender love for him had won
The praises of that surging crowd.
Their uncle told them as he fled
That all was lost, and death would be
The path through which the victor led
His army, 'till avenged was he,
So thoroughly was he impressed
By the dread issues of the day—
That with his family oppressed
With grief, he wouldn't for one moment stay.
So tenderly was Ianno
Impressed with her dear father's care,

She had not seen, nor did she know,
That Eyon was beside her there
With deep emotions looking on
Her pale, young, tender, anxious brow,
Trying to hide the tears she won
With all a child's affection now.
But when her father kissed away
The tears which trembled on her eyes,
And pointed to where Eyon lay,
She looked at him with strange surprise;
She knew not what to say or do,
Her throbbing heart could tell alone
The feelings which inspired anew
The love she dared not how to own.
Young Eyon felt embarassed too,
He knew not but she would repel
Her father's captor, if she knew
That it was by his hand he fell;
Had he not swept her father's power
Forever from the land away,
And left her in this very hour,
To all a captive's ills, a prey,
Those thoughts had crowded in his mind;
He felt her anguish in his soul,

And though she might yet think him kind,
How could he in her grief condole,
When he alone had wrecked the joy
Which courted her young happy years;
How could she love one who 'ld destroy
The peace which happiness endears.
Thus had he reasoned in his mind,
Whilst looking at the grief and woe
Which seemed the chieftain's heart to bind
In sorrow to young Ianno;
When in his seeming reverie
He heard Reginald call his name,
Then, with grave, modest courtesy
He introduced him to the dame,
" This is my daughter, Eyon," he said,
He knew that they before had met—
But seeing that they had yet delayed
Those friendly greetings which beget
True social feelings which impart
The friendship wove in memory—
He read the feelings of each heart
And thus effaced their misery—
With head uncovered Eyon stood,
As he reached out to her his hand,

His looks expressed a widowhood
Of joys bereft, he could not stand.
His agitated heart was felt
In that soft pressure which he gave—
Whilst her deep mine of young love's wealth
Her own expressive soul misgave.
" Sweetest lady," said he, " allow
The young man whom you did befriend,
His more than thanks here to avow
To you, with memories fond which lend
A hallowed peace of bliss and love
Around the influence of his soul
Like angels ministering above,
Where joys immortal minds control."
The softest ray of sunshine smile
Stole sweetly o'er her virgin brow
And chased the cloud of grief the while,
Which seemed to linger round it now.
" Your thanks, dear sir," she answered, " are
Accepted, let the past remain
Obscured in silence, why thus mar
Your triumph with one thought of pain."
She bit her lip in sorrow when
The sting she gave passed through his soul,

But he, the victor, and his men
There, held her father in control.
How could she in her heart confine
The sorrow of her father's grief,
Although her love might underline
Her very life, for that young chief—
Confused at her pointed reply,
He felt her sorrow all the more,
His love, his pride seemed to defy
Although he thought its influence o'er.
"Madam," he said, "your father's grief
With you in sympathy I share,
And though my triumph here is brief
It must not wound thee, lady fair."
"Dear Ianno," her father said,
"This brave young man we must not blame;
Had I my former power, instead
Of being estranged from where I came,
I would feel honored to have known
This gallant son of Erin's Isle,
Who has but justly claimed his own,
Although in royal princely style,
He has bestowed with generous heart
This castle and domain to me,

Here, with your father still thou art,
And little Rudolph, too, with *thee.
But here we must not linger on,
Let us into the castle go;
Come, Ianno, and you, my son,
Dispell your gloomy thoughts of woe."
That evening and the night were spent
In social bliss and harmony,
Whilst Eyon's happy †parents lent
Their presence to the company.
In spacious halls the soldiers too,
The social glasses seemed to share
Unmindful of their brothers who
Fell in that dreadful battle there.
All quaffed, and ‡chatted merrily—
In mythful glee time stole along

---

* These were the only two members left, of a family of a wife and eight children.

† Adrastus Eyon, early in the evening, withdrew from the party to his own home and induced his parents, after giving them a detailed account of the battle, to go with him to the castle on that occasion, which they cheerfully did, and enjoyed the event with pleasure.

‡ The Norman and Irish soldiers enjoyed themselves together in the same halls, and, strange as it may seem, they discussed the events of the day without any difficulty arising between them to mar the social harmony of the occasion. The Irishmen were instructed by their young leader, Eyon, not in any case to have any difficulty with the strangers, " who," he said, " in trying to speak what little they knew of the Irish tongue, might be led to say something they themselves, could not understand." The reader must be aware, that, for the last twenty-two years in the country, they had learned something of the language. They accordingly discussed matters with the Irish soldiers on this occassion, in their native Gaelic.

Whilst music and the revelry
Were blended in the voice of song.
Adrastus, lionized by all,
Too modest to receive their praise,
With Ianno, stole from the hall—
Then with a courteous smile, he says,
"Let us retire to yonder bow'r
Where we before as strangers met;
Ah! Ianno, that happy hour!
I never shall, or can forget.
My soul entranced with joys unknown,
Since then, has nursed its sweetness well;
That heart would be as cold as stone
Could it one happy thought repell."
"How can you thus," said Ianno,
"Allow your fancies to beget
Illusions which may come and go
Like sun-shine on the rivulet—
If one kind thought had smiled within
The peaceful sweetness of your heart,
Why did you leave on that night, when,
My uncle played a jailer's part?"
Within the bow'r he told her how
Her uncle tried to end his life,

And why the gods made him avow
Himself, to bring about the strife.
" Thus was I forced," said he, " to take
My exit from my lady friend,
And though my heart cannot bespeak
My love for her, could I attend
Her kind ministrations then,
When forced away by savage men.
Ah, Ianno! although it may
Seem strange the way we first have met,
And stranger still, how on this day,
When that dread conflict shadows yet
The peaceful sweetness which alone
Should bless the lover's heart with joy,
That we again should meet: I own,
This is an incident which I
Cannot divine, or understand,
Yet never was a heart so true
In this or any other land
Than that, which beats in me, for you.
And though I should not now avow,
This love which fills my very soul:
Yet in this place I cannot now
Its rising impulses control."

"Adrastus, though I must confess
The void occasioned in my heart,
Not being aware of your address
When on that night you did depart;
Yet circumstances now arise
Which place me in a lowly sphere;
Not in a stranger's sad disguise
Can I such declarations hear."
" Dear Ianno, how can you thus,
When you are not averse to me,
Forbid me such bliss to discuss
Which binds my heart and soul to thee.
Ah! smite not sweetest lady fair,
The life of one who would resign
The pleasures of this earthly sphere
To live in one pure thought of thine.
If you but bid me hope and live,
I shall grow happy in your smile;
Oh! say you will my past forgive
And memorize my love a while!
I know your tender heart may yet
Bestow that happiness to me.
Ah! dearest, let my love beget
But one sweet ray of hope in thee!"

" I could not try, no matter what
Reverses were in store for me,
To deny the influence that
Arises in my soul for thee.
And if my future years commend
A prospect worthy of your name,
Then, if you love me still, my friend,
None other can this poor heart claim."
With a devotion love alone
Could only feel or manifest,
He joyfully exclaimed, " my own ! "
Then, strained her to his manly breast,
A lover's kiss sealed on her brow,
The sweetness of his ecstasy—
His very soul seemed to avow
Its purpose of sincerity;
And though he bowed to her decree
To wait the time she would bestow
Her hand to him, yet happier he
Clung closer to his Ianno.
Back to the feast again they went,
Together with true, conscious pride,
Our hero happy and content
Leading his sweet, expectant bride.

The soldiers cheered them as they came
Into the banquet hall in view—
There, youth and beauty, pride and fame,
Seemed centered in those very two.
Throughout the night the rank and file
Enjoy'd the feast 'till dawn of day,
And though *Augusta felt the while
How mean her father skulked away—
Still, in her company McMore
A chatty, loved companion met;
And like a prince himself he bore,
Until he parted with regret—
But as he bid her the good-bye
She sweetly told him, call again—
The sparkle in her deep blue eye
Exposed her untold love within.
Young Eyon and his parents too,
Together with his soldiers all,
To Reginald bid peaceful adieu,

---

* Augusta and her mother, the daughter and wife of Rudolphus,
were at the banquet on that evening by special request of Reginald,
and introduced to young Eyon, who then introduced them to
McMore, his first and bravest officer. Augusta was charmed with
his princely bearing and manner, and so delighted him in return
that he became completely enamored of her. And, although she
felt the odium that must be cast upon her father at his disgraceful
and hasty flight, yet she felt relieved from her embarrassment under
the cultured care of McMore, to whom she was afterwards married
when her father returned to Inland.

And marched away from Castle Hall,
To that old *mansion which had been
The home of his dear parents when
Life's " honey-moon," they did begin—
He led them, and his gallant men.
Six months had scarcely passed away
When Castle Hall, illumined again
With brilliant lights, and grand display
Of ladies fair, and gentlemen
With courtly pomp and royal style
In that old castle, all aglow—
Young Eyon of green Erin's isle
Was wedded to his Ianno.
Another happy couple, too,
Linked with the golden chain of love,
The marriage ceremony went through—
Their mutual joys of bliss inwove
The deep affections which impressed
The sweetness of peace evermore,
Within the loving, happy breast
Of fair Augusta and McMore.

---

* After Adrastus Eyon bid adieu to Ianno and her father, he led
his soldiers and parents to a grand old stately mansion on the banks
of the Shannon, from which his father was driven twenty-two years
ago when the Norman invaders massacred, in cold blood, all the
other members of that illustrious family.

Another king* had ruled the throne
Of that old land of Normandy
Who restored Reginald to his own
Possessions in that country.
A golden future, full of fame,
And sweet ecstatic bliss smiled on
That gallant hero, whose proud name,
Is memorized in Poughlue Eyon.

---

* When Rudolphus quit the field of battle, after his signal defeat
by Adrastus Eyon. he was so completely demoralized on account of
his former wickedness, that he left the country in disgrace, without
scarcely bidding his family good-bye. In the disguise of a harper he
visited his own land, and found access to the young king, who was
but a few months previously placed on the throne of his fathers.
To him, after he impressed him with the sweetness of his music, he
told the story of his wrongs; and how he, together with his brother
Reginald, were driven from their possessions and forced to fly to a
foreign land,
    After the young Monarch had carefully listened to his story, he
restored him to all his lost rights, and directed him to go after his
brother to Erin. It was only when this announcement was made to
her father. by Rudolphus on his return, although she loved Eyon with
a passionate love, that she consented to become his wife.
    Her father, before his departure for his native home, and
Rudolphus, who was now forgiven for his former treachery, blessed
their union, as they did also that of Augusta and McMore, who were
married at the castle on the same night.
    It is needless to say, that the fruits of this matrimonial alliance
linked together the affections of those families in mutual peace and
harmony, and that a friendly intercourse for a long time after
existed between the two nations.

MISCELLANEOUS.

WASHINGTON'S TOMB.

The cypresses waving in grand ancient glory
Grow silently over the tomb of the brave,
And bear in their sombre impressions, the story,
Of national love, in the home of the grave.
Like sentinels weeping the nation's long loved
    one,
The grandest of heroes that nature has known;
They bend lowly over the urn, where lay on
The last mortal relics of immortal's own.

The ever green boughs of the cedar hang over
The tomb where our father of liberty lies,
And hide in their splendor of emerald cover
The citizen soldier whose name never dies;
The hallowed affections of sweetness entwine
'Round immortal glories enwreathing his fame
And gloriously guard all the virtues sublime
Which shine through the grandeur and pow'r
    of his name.

The forest oaks rising in old regal splendor,
Entomb in their shadows, our Washington's
    tomb,

Like proud crested monarchs, all anxiously
  tender
To grace with their presence the deep hallow-
  ed gloom,
A still, solemn silence eternally sleeping
Within his lone, encurtained, grave forest
  home,
In awful majesty companions its keeping
With impressive grandeur, beneath heaven's
  dome.

HELEN'S GRAVE.

Whilst Luna was shining through the darkness
  of night,
And the pale stars were twinkling with their
  silv'ry light,
I arose from my pillow and silently stray'd
To the grave, where my Helen untimely was
  laid.

I gaz'd on the head-stone 'till the tears made
    me blind
To think my beloved one I no longer could
    find,
Overpower'd with emotion my heart seemed to
    break
As I anxiously called on my Helen to speak.

Oh! why did you leave me, my beloved one
    alone,
When life is insipid and I live but to moan,
Should your ghost hover round me then sweet
    angel sprite,
Let me live for an hour once again in your
    sight.

How dear was that moment, when my love I
    first spoke,
What sweet nightly visions through my slum-
    bers broke
Like a stream undisturbed gliding fast to the
    sea,
Were my days of affection, when spent love
    with thee.

But, alas! I have lived to behold thee no more
Yet, thy image remains in my heart's inmost
    core,
Like a pilgrim I'll wander each lone hill and
    dale
And at night in my dreams I shall weep thy
    sad tale.

THE REPUBLIC OF THE WEST.

No nation ever proudly rose
To eminence and fame,
Where freedom's holy claim
Was gained from freedom's foes,
Than the Republic of the West
Where peaceful nature smiles to rest.

No country on this earthly sphere
With grander prospects can appear
To bless a nation's peaceful love
With God's own blessings from above,
Where majesty supremely grand,

Triumphantly walks hand in hand
With freedom's goddess, fitting mates
For these great famed United States.

Despotic monarchs find no place
There, to erect a bloody throne,
No kingly power through God's grace
Such false assertions there can own.
Those thoughts of superstitious pow'r,
Too long expressed in ages past,
Are fancies wild, estranged from our
Which manhood's rights shall ever blast.

The glory of God's love, divine,
Transmitting life to man,
Impressed his soul with thoughts sublime,
When manhood's years began.
The stamp of that eternal right
In proud Columbia's shore,
Shall show its dazzling brilliant light
Through ages evermore.

And though ambitions wild may school
Some upstart to forget,
The principles of freedom's rule,

In be'ng a monarch yet—
We'll wipe the fool's desires away
With freedom's bold behest,
And teach him to bow down, obey,
The NEW ROME of the West.

I FEAR I SHALL DIE AN OLD MAID.

I fear I shall die an old maid,
My young days are fast taking wing—
When lonely I walk on the glade,
Of sweet love, and Hymen, I sing;
At night, on my pillow I lay—
Sleepless, without ease or rest:
Discoursing of marriage all day
Enkindles a flame in my breast.

My passions I try to subdue,
But, ah! like the waves of the deep,
They follow each other anew,
And break on my mind as I sleep:
The pathways of love I traverse,
Where numbers of beaux I can see:

I sing to them rhyme and blank verse,
They seem to look kindly on me.

And often I'm called on to play,
When papa brings guests home to dine:
" Her music is charming," they say,
Yet, each thinks, she 's old to be mine.
Alas! how oft have I numbered
The thirty long summers I 've seen;
Reck'ning my years, I'm incumbered,
Why did I not wed at fourteen?

DINGLE BAY.

Beneath a clear sky, in a green lovely island,
Dame nature resides, her bright scenes to dis-
    play,
The astounding gods of the high topped Olym-
    pus,
Ne'er gaz'd on such beauties, as mark Dingle
    Bay,
The wild breakers rush from the foaming At-
    lantic,

Winding impetuously without delay,
'Till majestic cliffs raise their spray to the
    zephyrs,
To kiss the fresh breeze, which blows 'round
    Dingle Bay.
The responding echoes, resounding the notings
Of the feather'd warblers, whilst passing along,
Like magic deluding the judgment of reason,
The meandering waters each note still prolong.
The blythe, merry laugh of the youthful
    admirers
Is hushed, whilst the voice of the sages doth
    say:
The finger of God here, has painted a model,
For beauty surpassing surrounds Dingle Bay.

TO MY WIFE, ON HER 30TH BIRTHDAY.

The tide of youth may steal away,
As years roll o'er thy brow,
And sorrow for thy loved ones may
Thy heart's fond wishes plow;

14

But time or sorrow never can, those calm, mild
    looks destroy,
Love, virtue, grace and innocence, companions
    of thy joy.

A soul like thine, so pure, so mild—
'Tis sweetness nursing grace,
The image of the little child
Who walks before God's face.
The dimpling beauties of thy smiles are like
    the sunny beams,
Playing with the silent ripplings of the purest
    crystal streams.

THE ECCENTRICITIES OF DAVID REIDY.

A youthful student, first, we find
In little Mr. Reidy,
He grew in logic undefined,
Until his mind got seedy.

He master'd sci'nce, so people say,
Yet some are prone to doubt it;

He takes old rye instead of tay (tea),
Although quite well without it.

He factors fractions quite as well
As when he whipp'd the childer—
On fractions though, he cannot dwell,
His brain they soon bewilder.

As pedagogue, he flourish'd once,
Although his diction 's funny:
Yet none could dare pronounce him dunce,
His eyes appear so cunny.

He 's never angry, but times,
His jaws expand with rage:
At " forty-five " he bets his dimes,
And quotes each gambling sage.

TO MISS MOLLIE V. KAIN, ON HER SIXTEENTH BIRTHDAY.

Sweet rising star of womanhood,
What brilliancy is thine?

Enthroned in innocence and grace
Like angels looks, divine.
The peaceful hope of modesty
Sits calmly o'er thy brow,
There let it rest through future years,
Dear child, as well as now.

The blushing rose which decks yon bow'r,
When vernal spring has flown,
Assimilates that rosy tinge
Which nature calls thine own.
Those smiles which play with dimples soft,
Like sunbeams 'round thy face—
May they illume thy tender life,
Dear child, in every place.

MY MOTHER'S GRAVE I MOURNING SOUGHT.

My mother's grave I mourning sought,
No bosom friend was nigh,
But memories of absent days
Renew'd each tender sigh.

A weeping willow marked the spot
Where undisturb'd she slept;
My heart to fil'al love succumb'd,
In bitter strains I wept.

The grass grew long above her head,
That face I looked with joy,
Beneath the earth is mouldered now,
Why mother, did you die?

In pensive mood I listen'd for
The hearing of her voice,
As if the dead could answer me!
And make my heart rejoice.

I plucked the flow'rs, yet wet with dew,
And strew them on her grave—
That offering of innocence,
To her, with tears I gave.

ON THE DEATH OF THE RIGHT REV.
THOMAS FOLEY, D. D.

From God's own fold, where majesty
Enthroned in christian grace,
Bows down in adoration meek
Before the Savior's face:
A shepherd, sanctified in love—
A priest of the most high,
Is called to wear his crown above,
Where saints hosannas cry.

In charity, sweet peace, and faith,
His honored life was spent:
His language was the word of God—
That God to whom he went.
The love of truth and innocence,
Was nursed within his breast,
And like an angel's smile, from hence,
It coaxed him to his rest.

His voice is heard no more on earth,
But yet, its solemn tone
Shall vibrate like the vesper-bell
Through hearts where God is known.

The church bells tolled in measured tones,
His life on earth was run—
The last words spoken through his moans
Were, " God, thy will be done!"

THE OLD BACHELORS.

Behold the chagrin faces
Of men advanced in years,
Who gaze on pretty laces
On smiling little dears:
They're shocked to see, they're shocked to know
That women are so vain, so, so!—

Old bachelors, discarded men,
Filled with the thoughts of faded bloom,
Declare it is the wise man's "boom"
To keep aloof from marriage, when,
Within their minds, their passions swell,
To think they're left alone to dwell.

When at the the'tres they behold,
The young, the beautiful, the old,

Their hearts are filled with caustic spleen,
Whilst gazing on that human scene—
Then, criticising they express
Their notions of each lady's dress.

And if the play has ought of love,
Those ministers who look above
With holy visions in their eyes,
In prayer to God beyond the skies,
Could never picture men as well
As those who are left alone to dwell.

Yet in such quarters where love scenes —
And if they could, behind the screens:
They're always found in foremost places
With grins like gaping graves, their faces —
Admiring all with vain delight,
You gods immortal what a sight!

ALL-FOOLS' DAY.

All-Fools' Day, as some display
The mocking whims of foolish play,

Their social schemes, like happy dreams,
Impress the mind with joy, which seems
To steal their thoughts from thoughtful care,
Súrrounded by the toils of strife,
And nurse those pleasures wild which wear
An innocence of foolish life.

From years mow'd down by *Time's* dread
    scythe
Into the dark, engulfing past,
The story wings its magic pride,
Nor yet disdains to move aside,
But clings to old traditions fast,
When men of sense, as senseless tools
Of sentimental jokes, were fools.

The laughing crowds all gape and grin
When some device of boys or men,
Ingeniously is play'd upon
Some thoughtful, yet unconscious one,
Who passing through the jolly crowd—
Is hailed, " Fool! fool! " in accents loud.
In jokes of var'ous kinds the day
In peaceful mirth is passed away.

LINES WRITTEN AT THE REQUEST OF ONE OF THE MEMBERS OF THE ST. CECILIAN MUSICAL SOCIETY OF ST. COLUMBA'S SCHOOL.

Sweet music, heavenly voice enthroned
In love divine, thy hallowed tone
Enraps the soul in raptures wild,
As if its strains were bliss alone.
Cecilia, dear patron saint,
Of sweetest melody divine,
Entranced in fondest wishes told
We bow before thy sacred shrine.

Entrancing ecstasies untold
Of music sweet, long honored, sung
Like memories fondly which unfold
The peaceful joys, which round thee hung.
To thee we dedicate our muse,
Oh! blessed happy saint intone
Our modulations, and infuse
Our hearts with virtue like thine own.

TO J. D. SULLIVAN, ESQ.

Dear friend, as a patriot, soldier,
I greet thee and honor thy name,
The love of your country is holier
Than immortal glory, or fame—
For love is the offspring of heaven,
And next to God's glory alone,
Our country should always be given
The dearest affections we own.

The diamond possessing rare beauty,
Through matchless brilliancy shown,
Compares not with patriots' duty,
When flashes of love make it known.
Thy heart's treasured wishes inherit
That pride which led patriots on
To die for their freedom, and merit
True immortal glory, each one.

NO PASSIONS SHOULD ARISE.

No language of profanity should burst the lips
    of Man.
Nor vile impetuosity of any creed, or clan;
Devoid of immorality, in immodesty's disguise,
We should not break our Maker's law, nor let
    our passions rise.

Like the raging tide in motion oft wicked men
    contend,
In strife and disaffection fierce, against a foe,
    or friend,
And glide along life's stormy sea, forgetful of
    the prize
Awaiting every honest man, who lets no pas-
    sions rise.

No passion should assail the mind, or rule the
    soul within,
The former is temptation, and the latter one, a
    sin—
Temptation points to evil ways, whilst sin to
    heaven cries
In angry wand'ring exiles, who let their pas-
    sions rise.

Observe the course of wisdom then, and strife
    shall be no more,
The path is strewn with evergreens, and leads
    to virtue's door,
Where angel sprites, in calm delights, away
    beyond the skies,
Shall cheer each traveler homeward, who lets
    no passions rise.

ON THE DEATH OF MY BELOVED WIFE, MRS. KATE KAIN BREEN.

'Tis sad, my beloved one, 'tis sad to my heart—
'Tis sad to my soul, overburdened with woe,
To miss those sweet heavenly looks which
    impart
A sunshine of love through our cares here
    below.
The sweetness of peace which the blessed
    alone
In the glory of God's deep affection enjoy—

That sweetness of virtue and peace was thine
    own
The beauties of heavenly visions thy joy.

'Loved, dearest child! all their beauties rose
    'round thee,
The bright star of *Heavenly Hope* led thee on—
The sorrows of parting which hung thick
    'round me,
To thee were new glories thy virtues had won;
For the world's dark sorrow was left to
    impress
My sad heart estranged from thy love ever
    more,
Whilst heavenly angels come 'round to caress
Thy pure, tender soul with the sweetness they
    bore.

Oh time! overburdened with sorrows and woes,
Why nurse in the heart the delusion of peace
When mortal surroundings no blessings dis-
    close,
But God's love immortal when life's throbbings
    cease.

Farewell, my dear child! the deep wells of
    sorrow
Which flow through my soul shall remind me
    of thee—
Reflect in my lone heart the brightness you
    borrow
From God's holy presence, and oh! comfort
    me.

MARSHAL M. BENNER.

Of whom could I sing more deserving, I know
    not,
In the depths of my soul I would honor his
    name,
And twine 'round his memory the wreaths of
    affection
An immortalized tribute to his worth and
    fame.
A soul that is noble and pure lives within him
And counsels a mind, independent, sublime,
His majestic bearing, yet mild, gentle manner,
Imprints his name on the quicksands of time.

From modest retirement he reached distinction,
Respected alike by old, young, rich and poor,
His heart like a fountain flows on to the needy
Whenever their shadows fall over his door.
No false, haughty airs ever darken his visage,
Nor obscure his mind from his youth's inno-
  cence,
The greater his fame grows, the milder his
  manner—
No tongue can upbraid him with any offense.
Stem on, beloved chieftain, through life's ebb-
  ing ocean
Thy bark shall sail gloriously on to its end
'Till stranded on the shore of justice and mercy,
When God shall reward thee with blessings,
  my friend.

TO A FRIEND.
AN ACROSTIC.

Hail, youthful friend of cultured fame—
Extolled for logic, wit and lore:
Nestor-like thy pow'rs proclaim
Rich mines of knowledge yet in store.

Your genius, like the golden sunshine
Frescoing nature with its glow,
Demonstrates rare thoughts sublime
Ordained for classic minds to know.
No youth more favored near the goal
Of Demosthenean eloquence:
Vain thoughts or pride yet can't control
A man of such a noble soul,
Nor leave it stained with false imprints.

TO M. W. RYAN, ESQ.

Hail worthy son of honor'd sires
Distinguished in the sphere of man,
I greet thee with sincere desires
To sing thy praises, if I can.

The task is easy, all thy deeds
Are guilt with love from virtue's ray,
'Twas love of virtue sowed the seeds
When thy young heart was blight and gay.
15

The years of manhood strengthened all
Those passions nursed by grace divine,
The world's ways could never enthrall
A mind so pure, so good, as thine.

Speed onward, gallant son of fame,
May all your actions lead you on,
'Till ages shall your worth proclaim,
And love you as an honest man.

THE FLAG OF THE UNION.

Hail freedom's happy banner of Columbia's
    golden shore,
Distinguished among nations by the muses
    sung with lore,
Made dear by every virtue that honor could
    commend,
Thy glor'ous stars we love to see, thy stripes
    we shall defend.

A floating emblem in the air of peace and
    liberty,
A bold display of union and loyal sincerity,
Like a standard of perfection thy colors shall
    prove true,
Whilst millions shall proclaim the praise of
    the Red, White and Blue.

Untarnished by dishonor over cities waving
    high,
The banner of our happy land, for which the
    brave would die,
The patriots' devotion, and the emblem of true
    fame,
Lit up with stars of brilliancy emitting free-
    dom's flame.

Long may this glorious emblem of victory dis-
    play
Its stars and stripes for ever free from any
    tyrant's sway,
Th' insignia of our Union through ages let it be
The banner which shall proudly wave above
    the " brave and free."

TO THE MEMORY OF OUR FIRST BORN ELLEN ELIZABETH BREEN, WHO DIED AT THE AGE OF 3 YEARS AND 4 MONTHS, MAY 10th, 1873.

She died! the rosy tint of life stole gently from
    her brow,
Her mother's love, her father's smiles no more
    can greet her now;
Her calm, sweet looks of innocence shone forth
    through death's decree,
As if the heavenly angels wished to win her
    company.
She died, her eyelids closed in death, her lovely
    face was wan,
How sweetly beamed her last calm looks before
    life's setting sun,
Her little heart oppress'd, with weight, sunk
    gradually to rest,
Her painful motions ebb'd away, she mingled
    with the blest.

She died, her papa's darling child, her mam-
    ma's loving pet,
Lay still before our silent gaze, that face can
    we forget?

No never in this land of tears, whilst God our
    lives shall save,
In spirit we shall minister around her youthful
    grave.
She died! the angels called her home, her
    place was not on earth,
The smiles of heavenly graces, which were
    born at her birth,
She nursed with loving innocence awaiting
    God's command,
Then sighed upon this world of woes, and
    sought the happy land.

She died! her lovely features looked as calm in
    death's repose
As if the sweets of nature kissed the vernal
    spring's first rose,
In yonder silent grave she lies to mingle with
    the clay,
Which hides our darling child from us, and
    from the light of day.
She died! she lives to die no more in yon celes-
    tial sphere,
Where hosts of heavenly angels before their
    God appear,

Companion of those happy saints look calmly
    down and see
The hearts of deep affection which thy parents
    have for thee.

———

WHO ELSE COULD I LOVE?

———

Who else could I love, dearest maiden, but thee,
Every thought of my heart is thine own;
To thy tender soul I could peacefully flee,
With an angelic thought to dwell there alone.

In the smile of thy love e'er faithful and true,
My transit through life would be all but divine,
Let my hopes lead me on to the altar with you
And ever enthroned in my soul you'll be mine.

When love's fondest dreams are entrancing the
    soul
With ecstasies born of sweetness divine,
What mortal could once for a moment control
Their inherent glories, so pure, so sublime.

A MOTHER'S ELEGY.

FOR HER BABY BOY.

Written by request of Mrs. J. O'C.

He died! he calmly passed away
　　To yon celestial sphere,
To take the crown that angels wear,
　　My little baby dear.

'Tis sad to think his little smiles
　　No more can cheer my heart;
Oh, baby! lovely baby boy!
　　Why did you thus depart?

A father's burning love was thine,
　　For thee he knelt in prayer,
　　That God might guard thy future life,
From dangers everywhere.

But now, alas! like me, he weeps,
　　Although our tears are vain,
For little baby's playful smiles
　　No more with us remain.

He died, that little, sweet, calm brow,
　　Alas! shall never more
A mother's burning kisses feel
　　Such as it felt before.

And, oh! that little sweet laugh which
　　Indulged a mother's joy,
No more in playful sweetness thrills
　　Her heart, my darling boy.

But God that gives and takes away,
　　Then may His will be done;
In angel bliss for evermore,
　　Shall live my baby son.

DECORATION DAY.

O'er the graves of the dead where a year's
　　silence slept
The voice of the living respectfully breaks
In a chorus of love through the sadness which
　　wept

'Round the scene which the sweetness of
  strewn flowers awakes.
The sorrows and joys of a mind shadowed less
With sadness arising from sympathy's throne,
Ever wake in the heart a lone echoe's caress
For those lost ones we mourn so lonely, alone.

Sweet garlands of flow'rs over graves long
  neglected,
Are strewn with affection to honor the dead,
Whilst musical greetings life's joys have re-
  flected
With the grand intonations its sweetness have
  bred.
The wild, fierce strife of war has ceased its
  grim rattle—
The terrors arising from conflicts are o'er;
Those sad scenes engraved in each famed field
  of battle
Are pictures of love we should cherish the
  the more.

The glories of fame through the nation resounded
And swept its dread echoes all over the land;

The blue and the gray, like the Romans,
    astounded
The world with power as they fought hand to
    hand
Those brave, immortal heroes whose death we
    deplore
In the anguish of love's devotional bliss,
Shall appear in the annals of fame ever more
Though their mounds neglected our greet-
    ings should miss.

TO A FRIEND.

True friendship, the seed of affection,
Grows only in hearts that are true:
It fructifies under protection
Of manhood, John Sinnott, in you.

A heart ever faithful impresses
Its imprint of honesty too—
And here let me say it expresses
Its grandeur sublimely in you;

For here in this vale we discover
That all is not gold which doth shine,
Yet, dear friend, in true friendship ever
May friendly friends greet thee and thine.

THE FRIENDS OF OUR YOUTH.

*Dedicated to my friend and schoolmate, Thos. Hanifan,
Esq , East St. Louis.*

Dear Thomas, our school days together
    When Spring's merry whisperings of youth,
Like innocence playing on the heather,
    Were bright with love, sweetness and truth;
Those days I recall oft at leisure
    And think of the time when we met,
When the sunshine of peace, joy and pleasure,
    Shone round us; oh! can we forget.

The village school yet stands as proud as
    It did twenty years there ago,
When the master's birch-rod, dearest Thomas,
    Was all that we dreaded, you know;

And often influenced by its terrors,
　　We learned to drink deep of lore
To wash out the stains of our errors,
　　To save our poor hands from being sore.

The stream where we often went fishing—
　　The serpentine winding Shannow,
With golden trout always was blushing—
　　I wonder, dear Tom, if 'tis now;
Its crystallized waters were hallowed
　　With banks clothed over with green,
Whilst clifts here and there overshadowed
　　The smiles of its ripplings serene.

The green-mantled meadows we play'd on,
　　With bat and ball, eager to goal,
Were amusements of victories won
　　Which anchor their joys to my soul;
Their memories shall cling to me ever,
　　Dear Thomas, though tyrants there sway,
For the glories of Erin shine over
　　My life till it passes away.

LINES WRITTEN IMPROMPTU AFTER READING OVER A LADY'S ALBUM.

A lady's album oft reflects
    The minds of those who write,
Their names therein, to show how men
    Purline its virgin white.

The minds of some reflected thus
    Look triv'al, light and vain,
Ambition sees false hopes in these,
    In those an empty brain.

A dashing, swagg'ring hand looks well,
    When viewed without inspection;
But then the eye shall vainly try
    To see therein, perfection.

Some vain attempts to court the muse—
    Some witty phrases borrowed
Among its leaves, like beaten sheaves,
    Appear displaced and narrow'd.

Some crumped-up lines disorded run
　　Through many of its pages,
And represent the miser's stent
　　Through all his wretched stages.

A flourish here and there proclaims
　　Some " swell" with the high collar,
Who looks as if his neck was stiff
　　And never owned a dollar.

A bold, plain hand, shows free command,
　　A man without flirtation;
An able mind, respectful, kind—
　　A man of education.

Its pages are an index of
　　The vanities of the sex;
Its writings here and there appear
　　A rumbling human vortex.

THE MAIDEN'S FIRST WHISPERINGS OF LOVE.

The innocence glowing 'round the youth of
    life's morn
Had veiled from the heart all the bliss of its
    noon,
When love's happy treasures like rare bril-
    liants worn,
Are kissed by the soft, golden beams of the
    moon.
The ecstasies felt in the mind calmly hallow
The peace which sweet angelic whisp'rings
    impart;
When nature drinks deep of the virtues that
    borrow
The joys shining over the pure, tender heart.

The flow'rs softly blushing when summer's sun
    smiles on
Their fragrant perfections, so sweet to behold,
Are nature's gems wedded to modesty won
From beauties as bright as the hues they unfold.

Thus glow'ng with the first smiles of love
    beaming over
The brow of the lovely young maiden, she
    seems
Like a fairy enthroned in the bow'r of a lover,
When all his bright glories are pictured in
    dreams.

'Tis thus that the maiden entranced by the rap-
    tures
Of love stealing over her innocent soul,
Finds life an ethereal bliss which she captures
From thoughts fast arising she cannot control.
Its sweetness awakens new glories unknown,
Like joys overflow'ng from God's fountain
    above;
She breathes but the peace of its influence
    alone—
It is the young maiden's first whisp'rings of love.

www.ingramcontent.com/pod-product-compliance
Lightning Source LLC
Chambersburg PA
CBHW030818020726
47499CB00006B/1967